SEAL'S DEFIANCE

TAKE NO PRISONERS

BOOK #7

ELLE JAMES

New York Times & *USA Today*
Bestselling Author

Author's Note

Read other stories in the Take No
Prisoners Series:

Visit www.ellejames.com for more titles
and release dates

Also visit her alter-ego Myla Jackson at
www.mylajackson.com

and join Elle James and Myla Jackson's
Newsletter at
http://ellejames.com/ElleContact.htm

Dedication

This book is dedicated to the selfless doctors who give of their gifts to provide medical attention and services to the people who do not have access or money to pay for it. They brave the elements, civil wars and terrorists to do what they do best. Thanks, docs!

Escape with...
Elle James
aka Myla Jackson

Chapter One

"IT'S FUCKING GRAND CENTRAL Station in Samada tonight," Declan O'Shea muttered into his radio. On point for this mission, he studied the small village in semi-arid, southwestern Somalia. Either Intel had it wrong or the al-Shabaab leader, Emir Fuad Hassan Umar, had called a meeting of all his leaders, or he had beefed up his security in the past twenty-four hours.

"I count fifteen bogeys on the south corner." Swede had moved into position on the southern end of the village.

"Same on the north," Fish reported. "Tight perimeter as well. No one sleeping, yet."

"Over twenty stationed outside our target structure," Irish said from his location thirty yards from one of the grass huts on the east end of the village. He hugged the shadows, his night vision goggles pushed up on his helmet, unnecessary with the full moon lighting the sky like daytime. Not conducive to a surprise attack on the emir.

Orders were orders. Over two hours

ago, the eighteen-man team had fast-roped from the two Black Hawk helicopters several miles from the target. They'd moved in on foot, carrying the explosives and weapons they needed.

SEAL Team 10 had been tasked to decapitate the head of a growing al-Shabaab faction led by a murderous former member of the Somali Islamic Courts Union who'd wiped out entire villages of people. In one village, he and his men had gone through, hut by hut, and killed the men, raped the women and slaughtered the children. When they were through pillaging, they burned the structures to the ground. In other villages, he'd wiped out the entire population and strewn their corpses for the scavenger birds.

A freelance news reporter happened upon the scene shortly after. The pictures he'd sent back to be printed in the US and the UK newspapers had shocked the westerners. But not until the rebels raided a small women's college in a suburb of Mogadishu, kidnapped all the females and sold them into slavery, did the U.S. administration take action.

Langley did their magic with satellite images, and SEAL Team 10 got the alert to stand ready to deploy.

They hadn't known their destination until they boarded the C-130 aircraft bound for a joint forces post in Djibouti, on the Horn of Africa. They landed in Camp Lemonnier at night, were secreted into an operations building where they slept through the day and prepared for the mission to be conducted the following night. After a thorough briefing by intelligence officers, they loaded helicopters from the U.S. Army's 160th Special Operations Regiment, otherwise known as the Night Stalkers—the aviation unit known for its ability to fly helicopters fast, at low altitudes and under extremely hostile conditions. They had more balls than all the other pilots in the military and were the SEAL team's life line.

Intel had estimated thirty terrorists, not the fifty Irish counted with Fish's and Swede's numbers combined. Those were the figures they could *see* on the outside of the main building. The emir could have called a meeting of all of his subordinate leaders, and they could be gathered inside the building, plotting their next murderous raid.

The SEAL team was highly outnumbered, and the rebels were well armed, each carrying a semi-automatic rifle with thirty-round banana magazines and spares.

"Count on fifty to seventy rebels. Your call, Gator," Irish spoke softly into his mic.

The leader of their team Remy "Gator" LaDue's voice crackled through Irish's headset. "They have to sleep sometime."

That was the team's cue to wait and watch.

Irish got comfortable, tucked into a bush, his face blackened with camouflage paint, alert but conserving energy for the battle to come.

Slowly, the rebels settled in for the night, many of them lying in the dirt, weapons clutched in their hands.

An hour went by before the door to the target structure made of straw, sticks and mud opened, and men poured out. Ten loaded into nearby trucks and left, others collapsed onto the ground and talked for a few minutes before lying down to sleep. The village grew quiet.

Forty-five minutes later, Gator's voice came through, "Let's do this."

Irish crawled out of the bush, flexed his muscles and moved forward, shifting his finger to the trigger of his specially modified M4A1. His muscles bunched, his control tight on every movement. Surprise was as much a weapon as the rifle in his hands.

Ten yards before he reached the first perimeter guard hunkered against the side of a hut constructed of sticks, with a grass, thatched roof, Irish paused. The hairs on the back of his neck prickled. Something wasn't right. The ground around him was too clean, too clear. He dropped to his haunches and scanned the area. A thin glint of light alerted him to something shiny stretched between two bushes.

"Fuck! The perimeter is wired—" he said into his mic.

As the words left his mouth, a loud explosion ripped through the silence and shook the earth, spitting dirt and rubble into the air.

Irish flattened against the ground, his pulse slamming through his veins. The trip wire hung inches from his nose. The explosion had gone off to the south where Swede, Big Bird, Gator and Sting Ray were. Someone had tripped the wire.

Every rebel in the village leaped to his feet shouting, guns at the ready. The door to the target structure burst open, and more men ran out into the yard.

"Plan Bravo!" Gator called into Irish's headset.

Irish, Tuck and everyone else opened fire on the rebels in the village, taking out as many as they could to provide cover while Hank and Dustman carried out their part of Plan Bravo. Positioned twenty feet on either side of Irish, the two SEALs, half-hidden in the brush, came to their knees and fired off two high-explosive grenades from the M203A1 grenade launchers attached to their rifles, aiming for the hut at the center of the village. One landed short, the other hit. Both exploded with a bright flash.

Half of the team pulled back, heading for the helicopter pick-up point. Their communications man would have put in a call to the waiting Night Stalkers. The helicopters would be in position when the SEALs reached the appointed landing zone.

They just had to get there.

Irish, Tuck, Swede and Fish would be the last to bug out, providing cover fire for the others.

"Gator was hit," Big Bird said into Irish's headset. "I've got him."

"Get out of here," Tuck said. "We've

got your six."

Irish eased away from the village, firing as he went. The chaos of going from sound asleep to fully alert was wearing off the rebels. In full-defense mode, they fired back, strafing the darkness surrounding the village in hope of hitting their attackers.

Hunkering low to the ground, Irish ran, doing his best to hug the shadows of trees and bushes. With the moon shining brightly, the SEALs could see the enemy, but the enemy could see the SEALs as well, especially when they were on the move.

Less than a mile away, the thumping sound of rotors whipping the air gave Irish incentive to pick up the pace. His teammates sounded off as they boarded the helicopters.

After one chopper filled, it left the ground and headed north toward Djibouti.

Irish could see the outline of the other chopper, the blades stirring dust in the air, whipping leaves and grass like an impatient child ready to leave.

"Come on, Irish," Tuck urged.

The words, barely audible over the pounding of his pulse against his eardrums, gave Irish incentive to pick up the pace. Rifle fire erupted behind him, the thunk of bullets hitting the dirt around him was even more compelling. He gave up zigzagging to avoid catching a bullet and ran full out, leaping aboard the helicopter.

He hadn't even gotten in when the aircraft left the ground, rising up into the air. Tuck grabbed him by his gear and dragged him all the way in the fuselage. Irish sat up and turned toward the open door. Even though he was inside, he wasn't safe yet. The door gunners on both sides fired onto the rebels below.

When the chopper was only fifty feet off the ground, a flash of light below made Irish's blood run cold.

The door gunner barely had time to yell, "Incoming!" when the helicopter gave a violent lurch and spun to the left, tilting precariously, losing altitude at an alarming pace. The pilot attempted to compensate and the craft lurched to the right before it hit the ground.

Irish slid across the floor, scrambling for purchase, his hands finding none. He tumbled out the open door, bounced off the skid and fell twenty feet, landing on his back in a pile of rubble of what had once been a hut. Stunned, with the breath knocked out of his lungs and his vision blurring, Irish watched as the helicopter pitched back to the left, flew another half mile, shuddered and crashed to the ground.

His heart banging against his ribs, Irish tried to rise. Pain shot through the back of his head, and he collapsed. Like a candle's flame in the wind, the moonlight snuffed out.

Dr. Claire Boyette hunkered in the shadows of the underbrush half a mile away from the village of Samada, listening to the sounds of gunfire. She prayed the rebels were shooting each other, not the remaining villagers who'd been forced to give up their homes for the rebels' use. Granted it went against her Hippocratic Oath to wish ill health on another human, but she didn't care. Umar and his thugs had done more damage to the nation than any other rebel faction, and they deserved to die a terrible death.

As soon as a lookout spotted Umar's trucks headed their way a week ago, Claire and her Somali counterpart, Dr. Jamo, had gathered as many of the women and children as they could and hidden them in the brush. Rather than just passing through, Umar and his treacherous entourage rumbled into the grass hut village and took over.

Claire and Dr. Jamo had established a small camp a mile and a half away from the village, off the main road and deep in the brush. They set up makeshift tents with the blankets they scavenged when the rebels weren't looking. But the only source for clean water was in the village. They couldn't keep sneaking in and out in the early hours of the morning without being caught.

That was a week ago, and now the rebels had appeared to be quite settled. Until gunfire erupted, and the sounds of men shouting could be heard all the way to where Claire had dared to lay down her head to sleep.

She had Dr. Jamo hurry the women and children deeper into the brush, abandoning their tents to hide behind bushes and trees in case the rebels came their way. Once her charges were well hidden, Claire crept toward the village, staying far enough away she wouldn't catch a stray bullet. She hoped. Her fear was for the welfare of the other villagers who'd been forced to stay and had been sneaking food and water out to the others. As a medical doctor, she wanted to be nearby to help those injured in the shooting.

As she neared the village, the gunfire increased and the thumping sound of a helicopter's blades churned the air. Rethinking her decision to check out things in the heat of a battle, Claire had started to turn when a helicopter left the ground and flew over the top of her head. From its shape and the guns mounted on each side, she'd bet it was an American Black Hawk. She'd seen enough of them when she'd passed through Camp Lemonnier, before she made her way into Somalia a month ago. Though the aircraft had gone, the thumping sound of rotors hadn't ceased.

Claire leaned around a bush and spotted another chopper in the distance as it rose from the ground and headed her direction.

A flash streaked from the ground nearby and was followed by a loud bang. The aircraft shuddered and the blades dipped to one side.

Claire tensed. Instinct made her duck, even though the helicopter flew well over her head. But not for long. Apparently, the chopper had taken a hit and was going down. As it tipped back the other way something...or someone ...fell to the ground within twenty yards of where Claire hid.

By the shape she could see in the moonlight, it was a man. She rose from her position, and started toward the spot where he'd landed. Before she'd gone five feet, the helicopter crashed into the ground half a mile away with a loud crunching of metal. The blades broke off and sliced through trees.

Claire hunkered low and kept running toward the downed man.

The rebels cheered, loaded into trucks and raced from the village to the fallen aircraft, headlights piercing the darkness.

Flames rose from the crash site and another explosion rocked the ground beneath Claire's feet.

Keeping close to the shadows of trees and bushes, Claire arrived at the spot she thought she'd seen the man fall. At first, all she could make out was the charred remains of a mud and straw building that had long been burned to the ground. Outside the village, it had probably belonged to a shepherd. Now the hut was nothing but a jumble of grass, rocks and sticks.

Claire glanced all around and was about to give up and hide herself when she heard a moan.

The trucks with the rebels would be near her position any minute.

To the side of a large pile of the rubble, lay a dark figure. Claire crouched beside him and checked for a pulse by pressing two fingers to his neck. If she had time, she'd unbuckle his helmet and loosen his bulletproof vest. But she didn't, and he didn't have the time for her to do anything but kick, scrape and rake rocks and bramble over his body, hiding him from view of the rebels, should they pause to check out the remains of the hut.

Claire did the best she could before throwing herself into the brush behind a large bush. There she lay, breathing as quietly as she could.

Men carrying guns tromped past the burned-out shell of the structure, barely glancing in the direction of the man half-hidden beneath rocks, brush and sticks.

As soon as the men went by, Claire returned to the man in black, aware more rebels would be headed their way. She had to do a better job of hiding the soldier or risk him being discovered.

Irish floated in and out of consciousness. Each time he tried to sit up, pain shot through his head, his vision clouded and he slipped back into an abyss of nothingness. Several times a pale feminine face hovered over his, surrounded by blue-tinged, light-colored hair. Cool fingers pressed to the base of his throat. "Did I die?" he whispered, his voice barely audible.

"Shh." She pressed a slim finger to his lips.

He puckered, kissing the pretty lady's finger. "Are you an angel?" Was it against the rules to kiss an angel? He didn't care.

"You have to be silent," his angel said. "Lie very still." She pushed rocks and brush over his body.

Irish blinked in and out, disturbed that his angel seemed intent on burying him. A stab of pain ripped through his head again, and he winced. "Dead sure hurts a lot."

"You're not dead," she assured him.

Though the SEAL in the back of his mind echoed *death was the easy way out*, none of his muscles responded to do anything about it. He lay as still as a dead man, slipping back into the blackness.

On another trip up to consciousness, moonlight barely came to him through the leaves and branches piled on his face. He lay on the hard ground, rocks and bramble digging into his back, his body covered in dirt, branches and grass. The earthy smell of dirt and dried leaves filled his nostrils. Again, he attempted to sit up, but the weight of his own body and the rubble covering him was more than he could lift.

In the back of his mind, he knew there was something he should be doing. A task both dangerous and urgent. If only he could stand, grab his weapon and move. Again, he slipped away, waking only when he felt hands on his chest and legs.

He tried to raise his arm to block the attack, but he couldn't make it move. It was as though a heavy weight had settled over his entire body. He was helpless to move and not conscious enough to protest.

"Lie still," the angel's voice whispered into his ear, her breath warm against his skin.

He blinked open his eyes and stared up into dark pools of indigo. There she was again, the woman who'd visited him before. He wanted to know her name. He opened his mouth to ask, but the pain knifed through his head, and he moaned.

"Shh. You must be quiet, or we'll be caught," his angel whispered.

"Kiss me." His head and body ached, and his vision grew more blurred. "Please."

"If you promise to be quiet."

He blinked once. "SEAL's honor."

She bent and pressed her lips to his.

He smiled, the pain receding for a moment, warmth stealing over him at her touch. She truly was an angel of mercy.

The sounds of footsteps and equipment rattling nearby disturbed the night.

"Lie still," his angel repeated. She covered his face with a branch and disappeared.

If he died now, at least he'd go having been kissed by an angel.

Chapter Two

CLAIRE SUFFERED through several groups of rebels passing near her location. Between each group, she scurried over to her soldier and rearranged the brush he'd disturbed.

He was restless and in pain, but she could do nothing about it until she moved him out of danger.

Thankfully, the rebels on foot and in trucks were more intent on reaching the downed helicopter. Apparently, they hadn't been close enough to notice the man who'd fallen out before it crash-landed. They concentrated their search efforts on finding the other souls on board the doomed aircraft.

As another group of al-Shabaab fighters passed through, Claire flattened herself to the ground and lay as still as possible. They trickled through, some moving faster than the others. All carrying guns.

A shout rose up from the men who reached the helicopter first and the others ran to catch up. Gunfire erupted, along with shouting. But there were not screams of pain and the gunfire seemed to be an unloading of weapons into the darkness, the rapid firing indicating the men were strafing the area. Claire hoped that meant the crew and passengers of the helicopter survived the landing and disappeared.

Time passed, and some of the men returned to the village, past the location where Claire and the downed military man lay.

Soon, all was still.

Claire assumed the rebels had given up finding the other occupants of the helicopter. They hadn't dragged any past her location. More than likely, they had assigned men to guard the crash site in case the passengers returned to destroy the craft.

After approximately thirty minutes had elapsed and no one passed her position, Claire took a deep breath and left her hiding place. This might be her only chance to move the man, if he could stay conscious enough to get to his feet and walk, assuming he wasn't paralyzed from landing on his back.

Hunkered low, she edged toward the crumbled wall of the structure and searched left and right. The moon was making its descent into the western sky, casting long moon shadows over the ground. Nothing moved.

Claire turned and quickly removed

the branches, rocks and rubble from the soldier's body. When she'd cleared him, she checked his pulse again. She held her breath until she could feel the strong, steady beat. Pressing a finger to his lips, she shook his shoulder and bent close to his ear. "Hey. Wake up."

He didn't move.

Her heartbeat kicked into high gear. The longer it took to revive him, the more chance of being found. Though doing so went against her grain, she braced herself to get tough. With the palm of her hand, she lightly slapped his cheek.

A hand shot up and snagged her wrist in a punishing grip.

"I wouldn't do that again, lass," he said, his voice low, dangerous. Her soldier's eyes were open and fierce.

A burst of fear shot through Claire. In the strength of his grasp, Claire figured he could easily snap her wrist. She didn't know this man, who he was, what he was capable of or his intentions toward her. If he became fully functional, she would be at his mercy.

Swallowing the lump of panic in her throat, she gave him a stern look. "Good. You're awake. If you want to stay alive, you have to move. And above all, keep quiet."

"Sure we can't stay put? I've a helluva

headache."

The hint of what sounded like an Irish or Scottish brogue made Claire's insides curl in a delicious way. She'd noticed it the first time he'd spoken. Now it was more prevalent. That plus the residual tingling of her lips where she'd kissed his added up to make her wonder if she was ill or simply attracted to the man. None of it would matter if she didn't get him out of this spot in a hurry.

What worried her most was that the fall from the helicopter could have resulted in a spinal injury. Moving him might paralyze him for life. On the other hand, leaving him where he was would be a death sentence. In broad daylight, the rebels would find him all too soon. Paralysis would be the least of his worries.

Claire prayed his spine was uninjured as she took his hand and pulled him to a sitting position.

He swayed and blinked. "Where am I?" he said, his voice low enough she could hear, but hopefully the sound wouldn't carry far.

"Outside the al-Shabaab-held village of Samada."

He unstrapped his helmet and took it off. "What happened?"

"You fell out of a helicopter." She looped his arm over her shoulder. "Right before the helicopter crashed."

Muscles tensed, he lurched forward, attempting to rise, nearly pushing her over in the process. "Have to get to my team."

"The rebels are looking for them, but haven't come through here with anyone yet. I assume the occupants made it out and are gone. We have to get out of here before they find you." Claire braced her feet and held on as he straightened and found his balance.

Voices sounded in the distance, growing louder, making Claire's pulse leap. "Someone's coming."

"Wait," he said. "Where's my rifle?"

"We don't have time to find it." She wrapped an arm around his waist and started forward.

Her patient didn't move. "Get my helmet," he said. "Can't risk them finding it."

Barely balancing the man with one hand, she scooped the helmet off the ground and headed for the goat trail leading into the brush.

The man leaned heavily on her, staggering like a drunk.

Claire prayed he would stay upright until she could get him far enough away from the rebels and the downed helicopter.

He swayed and almost toppled before

they'd gone fifteen yards.

The voices behind them were nearly to the rubble where Claire and her soldier had been.

"Get down." Claire eased him to the ground.

His legs buckled and he dropped to the earth, making no more than a whisper of noise.

Claire rolled her charge behind the dense foliage and then peered back the way they'd come.

Two rebels with their rifles slung over their shoulders stopped beside the crumbled wall. Though Claire understood a little of the native Somali language, they were talking too fast. They mentioned something about their leader Umar being angry. But that was all she got out of their conversation.

One shook a cigarette out of a pack and handed it to the other. A match was struck, making a small flame in the night sky. The tip of a cigarette glowed to life, and the match was tossed onto the pile of leaves and rubble where the soldier had been lying moments before. Immediately, the match flame caught on one of the dried leaves creating a small fire.

The rebel nearest to the match stepped on the flame, putting it out. Then he leaned down, lifted something out of the dirt and held it up to the moonlight.

Damn. A knife. It had probably fallen out of one of the soldier's pockets.

The discovery made the two rebels excited, and they talked even faster, bringing their guns off their shoulders and into the ready position. One switched on a flashlight, and both men made a three-hundred-sixty degree turn, shining the beam into the brush.

Claire flattened herself to the ground, closing her eyes to a mere squint.

The taller of the two rebels strode toward the goat trail, his gun pointed, his finger on the trigger.

Her breath caught in her throat, Claire remained hidden, not moving so much as an eyelash as the rebel started toward her.

She could see his legs through a gap in the bushes and trees. Five more feet and he'd be able to see them.

The soldier lying on the ground beside her tensed.

She eased a hand over his shoulder.

A shout from farther away made the rebel turn and retreat down the trail and back to the ruins where his buddy waited.

Not in the clear yet, Claire stayed down until the two were joined by three others and the five of them headed toward the crash site.

For a long moment, she lay still, breathing in and out slowly, calming her racing heart. When she thought the coast was well and truly clear, she leaped to her feet and leaned down to the soldier. "Come on, mister."

"Irish."

"Irish what?" she asked.

"My name."

"Well, come on, Irish." Again, she looped his arm over her shoulder.

He let her pull him to his feet and lead him away from their hiding place.

The going was slow, and by the time they neared the refugee camp, Claire's back ached. Irish leaned on her so heavily, she thought she might lose him before they arrived.

As tired as she was, she couldn't just dump him in the camp and ask for help. She had to get him to her tent located on the edge of the makeshift village and hide him. Fortunately, she'd insisted on her tent being set up at a little distance from the others, claiming the location would help her stay healthy to better treat the sick and injured.

Circling as wide a path as she could, she approached her tent from the rear, flung open the flap and half-dragged, half-walked Irish inside where she eased him to the floor. Claire bent over him. "Are you still with me?" she whispered.

No response.

Again, she pressed fingers to his neck, her own heart standing still until she felt the steady beat of his pulse. Then she collapsed on the floor beside him and rested her strained back and arms. She wasn't done. Sunrise would come soon, and she had to hide Irish in the small confines of her tent.

Once the burning in her arms and back subsided, she moved her cot, folding desk, medical supplies and equipment from one side of the tent and made a makeshift pallet of a sleeping bag and several blankets. Then she strung her mosquito netting from the ceiling, providing a little bit of a visual barrier for anyone peeking in through the door of the tent. When she had the pallet the way she needed it, she pushed, shoved and rolled Irish onto it.

He muttered and moaned but helped a little. Finally on the padded surface, he passed out again.

Claire found her penlight and shined it into his eyes. His pupils didn't respond correctly, indicating a possible concussion. Not much she could do for him. If he had swelling on the brain, she wouldn't be able to help him without the tools she'd need to drill a hole in his skull to allow excess fluid to drain.

Her fingers flew over the buckles, velcro, zippers and buttons of his flack vest, jacket and trousers as she stripped him enough to check for other injuries. Rolling him onto his side, she found a large bruise on his back and hip. His trousers were cut clean through on his left shin, a four-inch-long gash laid open his skin to germs and infection.

To keep from removing the trousers all together, she cut a small length at the ankle and ripped the trouser leg upward. Claire went to work on the abrasion, cleaning it thoroughly with her supply of boiled water. When she had dirt and grit out of the wound, she poured on alcohol to kill any germs and covered it with gauze and medical tape. Using the precious penicillin she'd stored in her kit, she gave him a shot to his derriere. It was the best she could do in primitive conditions, a fact she had long ago accepted when working with the Somali people. Food and shelter meant more to them than medical necessities. Infant mortality was high, and the rebels made sure all ages of mortality stayed at an elevated level.

When she was finished checking him over, she left him on the pallet and went to work rearranging the rest of the tent to hide him. She pushed her cot up next to him, positioned her boxes of medical supplies in stacks beside her cot and her desk in front of the boxes. Anyone looking into the tent would see her cot before they saw the pallet on the floor, and assume she'd built the barricade for more privacy.

At least that's what Claire hoped. When Irish was well enough to move, he'd have to be moved in secrecy.

And then what?

She hoped to hell he had some ideas. A week ago, when the rebels had taken control of Samada, they'd confiscated the ancient Land Rover Claire had purchased in Djibouti. No one had expected them to barrel into town, waving guns and firing into the air, until they'd arrived.

Rather than risk being taken by the rebels, Claire had walked away from her only form of transportation. For the past two weeks, she'd hidden on the edge of the quickly established refugee camp. The rebels knew about the refugee camp and sent over armed fighters to scare them once to remind them who was in charge.

Umar, their leader, had killed the elder of the village, cut off his head, driven a spiked rod through it and planted it in the earth as a reminder to those who turned against him.

Claire kept that in mind, knowing if she were caught harboring one of Umar's enemies, she'd be treated the same, even though she was a doctor and a member of the World Health Organization. Her backers could do nothing when she was at Umar's mercy. Vowing to move Irish as soon as possible, she finished rearranging her meager belongings.

Early in the predawn hours of morning, she crawled onto her cot, pulled the mosquito netting around her and the pallet, and laid a hand on Irish's muscled, bare chest. It moved evenly up and down. Occasionally, his uninjured leg jerked and his head moved back and forth, as if he were living a nightmare over and over.

Leaving her hand on his chest, Claire closed her eyes. Though the night had been trying, the morning and daylight would bring a whole new set of challenges. Hoping a visit from the rebels wasn't one of them, Claire fell asleep.

In the gray light of morning, Irish opened his eyes to a splitting headache and stared up at a curtain of light mesh hanging over him. If he turned his head just a little, sharp pain ripped through his skull. But the view of the pretty sandy-blond-haired woman, lying in the cot above him, made him forget the pain for a moment.

Lying on her stomach, she dangled her hand over the edge of the cot onto his chest and the side of her face was half over, as well. Her straight hair lay in disarray around her shoulders and across her cheek.

Had he imagined those soft, rosy lips kissing his?

Irish raised a hand to brush the hair from her cheek, the effort costing him in a stab of pain through his temple and across his skull. His back ached and, when he moved, his left leg joined the rest of his body in soreness. He felt like he'd been put through a meat grinder.

Slowly, the events of the previous day came back to him—the preparation, the explosion, grenades launched into Umar's hut, running for the chopper and the aircraft taking a hit.

His pulse sped, and he started to rise.

The hand on his chest applied pressure, holding him down.

Irish's gaze shifted from her lips to soft, gray-blue eyes.

"You're awake," she whispered.

"I have to get out of here." Again, he started to rise.

Her hand remained on his bare chest, and she shook her head. "It'll be daylight soon. I snuck you in last night. If you run out of here now, someone will see you."

"I'll take my chances," he said, sitting up.

"You might be willing to risk your life, but it's the others who will also bear the brunt of your discovery."

"What others?"

"We're on the edge of the refugee camp containing the women and children of Samada lucky enough to escape before the al-Shabaab rebels took over. So far, they haven't attacked us, but that could only be a matter of time. If they discover you among us, they'll kill everyone here."

"I have to leave. My team needs me."

"Your team is gone."

Irish tensed. He seemed to remember her saying something like that before, but hadn't quite grasped her meaning through his haze of pain. "I don't understand."

She slid off the cot and sat cross-legged on the floor in front of him and, keeping her voice down, she filled him in. "You fell out of the helicopter. It crashed. The rebels converged on it, but I didn't see them dragging any bodies back to Samada for the usual torture and dismemberment."

Some of his tension eased. If the rebels hadn't dragged them back to Samada, dead or alive, his team had gotten away. For a long time, he stared into her eyes. The woman had saved his life. She had no reason to lie to him.

"For today, you have to stay inside my tent, be quiet and not let anyone else know you're here." Her brows rose. "Understood?"

His lips twitched. He wasn't used to taking orders from a civilian, but he didn't really mind when it was his guardian angel. "On one condition."

She frowned. "You're not in a position to make conditions."

The way her nose wrinkled made his insides feel all tingly. Bossy and sassy. He liked this woman. Irish winked, the effort costing him another twinge of pain. "I only want to know the name of the lass who rescued me." He laid on the Irish accent he'd learned from his mother.

Her face brightened and the crease in her forehead lifted as she held out her hand. "Claire Boyette."

"And why in the hell are you in Somalia?"

She smiled. "I'm here as part of *Medecins sans Frontieres*." She grimaced. "Doctors Without Borders."

"A doctor, are ya?" He pinched the bridge of his nose before staring across at her. "Isn't it too dangerous for you to be here? Couldn't you go to Kenya or South Africa?"

31

"Samada was fairly safe until two weeks ago when Umar decided the village suited his army's needs and forced the people out."

"Why, my angel, didn't you leave then?"

Her lips twisted. "While I was herding women and children into the woods, Umar and his men confiscated my transportation. Unless I walk out, I'm kind of stuck. Besides, I have patients to tend in the hospital tent we were able to move. I couldn't leave them."

Irish started to shake his head, regretting it as soon as he did. Instead, he pinched the bridge of his nose again. "You're in grave danger."

"So far, I've stayed out of sight of the rebels. They're more interested in staging raids to other cities and villages than to fool with a bunch of women and children living in the woods."

"Still, you're in danger, here."

"Yes, but I'm a doctor. They are less likely to kill me than kidnap me. Trust me when I say that you are a bigger threat to me and the people in this camp. Umar has leveled entire villages for harboring his enemies." She pulled a penlight from beneath her pillow. "Stare straight ahead."

He did as she said, while she shined the light in both of his eyes.

Claire's gray-blue gaze stared into his intently. Her nearness made him more aware of the way she smelled of the outdoors and sunshine, and the way she bit on her lip when she concentrated. Yes, this doctor was having an effect on him, and he was in no shape to do anything about it. Even if he were, she probably would slap the stupid off his face for even trying.

"So, Doctor Claire." He paused, waiting for her to finish.

"Yes?" She switched off the light and stared at him with a clear direct look.

"Are you married?"

Her eyes widened and then narrowed. "What?"

"I meant to ask, will I live?" Irish glanced at her hand. No ring. No white band from where a ring might have been.

"Your pupils are responding, which is a good sign." She put the penlight in her pocket, pushed to her feet and stretched. "And no."

"No, I'm not going to live?" He grinned.

"No. I'm not married." She stepped out of the little room made of boxes and the tent wall. "Close your eyes. I need to change and get ready for rounds and clinic duties."

"I can help."

She appeared at the end of the pallet and dropped down beside him on her knees. Claire gripped his arms and said in a stern whisper, "No matter what, you are not to step foot outside this tent. And not a peep out of your mouth. Don't move anything or knock anything over." She let go of his arms and sat back on her heels. "Understood?"

He nodded, loving the way her eyes sparkled when she got all wound up. But stay still all day? "What am I supposed to do?"

"If you know what's good for you, you'll sleep away the day. If you're feeling better and the leg wound isn't infected, you have to get out of here, tonight." Again, she pushed to her feet. "Now, be nice and close your eyes." She turned away, grabbed the hem of her dirty T-shirt and tugged it over her head. Standing in nothing but her shorts and a bra, she wet a washcloth and performed a quick ritual of washing her face, neck, arms and torso, pushing the cloth beneath her bra. Claire glanced over her shoulder and glared. "Your eyes are supposed to be closed."

"Sorry, got something in one." What he'd gotten was a glimpse of a beautiful woman with a long lithe form and curves in all the right places. "Got it." He closed his eyes long enough for her to turn back

34

around, and then he opened them again.

Claire reached into a suitcase, pulled out a clean shirt and slipped it over her head.

Irish sighed. "A shame to cover such a lovely body."

She turned and threw the cloth at his head. "You are no gentleman."

Shaking his head, he raised his hands. "Never said I was. But you're all lady."

Her cheeks reddened as she dragged a brush through her long, straight hair until all the tangles were smoothed. Then she bent at the waist and gathered her hair into a single ponytail and cinched it in place at the crown of her head with an elastic band. She stood, and the ponytail made her look much younger than her years, but no less beautiful. Her hair pulled tightly back from her face emphasized her high cheekbones and full lush lips.

Lips Irish would like to kiss again.

"Was it my imagination or was I kissed by an angel last night?" he asked.

The color in her cheeks deepened. "I'm sure you were dreaming."

"Kiss me so I can compare with my dream."

"I will not." She pulled a white smock over her T-shirt, stuffed her stethoscope in the pocket and headed for the front tent flap. "Remember, no one must see or hear you."

Irish moved to sit on the cot as Claire left the tent, pulling the flaps tightly closed behind her. His head still hurt like hell. He raised his hand to the back of his neck and felt the goose-egg-sized lump at the base of his skull. Much as he hurt all over, he was lucky to be alive. Being so close to the town he and his team had been sent to annihilate, he wondered if he'd live long enough to get out.

Though danger lurked, he couldn't help but think about the pretty doctor out here in the middle of hostile territory. When he left, he'd have to convince her to go with him. He couldn't leave her knowing Umar might find out she'd harbored one of the American SEALs sent to kill him.

Chapter Three

AFTER HURRYING through her rounds in the makeshift hospital tent, Claire prepared a breakfast of military MREs and headed back to her tent. Butterflies fluttered in her belly and she found herself a little short of breath at the thought of seeing Irish, with his sexy accent and exceptional body.

She pushed through the flap and closed it behind her. Turning, she glanced at the wall of boxes. Nothing stirred, no sounds, no sign of Irish.

Her heart thumped in her chest, and she hurried around the boxes to find Irish lying on his back, his hands behind his head. "I thought you would never come back," he said, his voice hushed. "I'm bored out of my mind."

"Sorry, but it's necessary. My contacts tell me Umar survived the attack, and his men are on the hunt to find the occupants of the helicopter."

A frown pushed Irish's brows together. "I really need to be out there. If my team needs help..."

"You'll be no good to them dead." Claire handed him the packet of food. "I thought you could do with something to eat to keep up your strength."

Irish grimaced. "Thanks. I think." He took the offering and a plastic fork, patting the ground beside him. "Sit with me."

His smile made her want to sit right beside him and forget there was a world out there. "I should go."

"Please."

"Okay, but only for a minute. I'll be missed by my partner, Dr. Jamo."

"Is he American, like you?"

"No, he's Somali."

Irish tore into the green packet of food. "Where did you get these?"

"They were a donation from the base at Djibouti. Beats eating what the locals have. I'm here to help, not take the meager amounts of food they are able to grow themselves. Not only did Umar take over their village and kill the elders, he allows his men to consume what food the people had managed to store, as well as their livestock and what they were in the process of raising in their gardens. These people are destitute."

"That's probably why we were sent in to take him out."

"We being?"

"Navy SEALs."

Her heart stuttered. No wonder his

muscles were rock-solid and well-toned. The man could probably chew nails and spit them out without breaking a tooth.

Her eyes widened. "Nothing but the best to take out the rebels? It's too bad you didn't get here sooner. Before these people lost everything they owned." She pushed a strand of hair out of her face.

"What about you? Why Somalia?"

She smiled. "Africa is part of me. I actually grew up in Africa. My father is American, my mother French. They met here."

"Are they doctors or missionaries?"

Her smile slipped. "Doctors. They met when they worked together on a cholera outbreak in Ethiopia thirty years ago. My parents fell in love with the people and the beauty of Africa, and with each other. They chose to remain in Africa to raise me and help people who had little access to medical care."

"Very altruistic."

Her back stiffened. "They cared deeply about the people."

He touched her arm. "Apparently they passed that down to their daughter. Where are your parents now?"

"They died in a bush plane accident."

"I'm sorry to hear that."

"It's been a while." Claire glanced at her hands, a lump forming in her throat as it usually did when she thought of her parents.

When Claire had turned fifteen, she was shipped back to the States to live with her paternal grandmother and attend a public high school in Iowa. There she'd been bored, barely socialized with the other students she had nothing in common with, and poured herself into her studies. Graduating Valedictorian, she'd been accepted into Harvard where she completed her undergraduate degree in pre-med Biology.

Her grades and MCAT scores got her into Johns Hopkins. Determined to finish her education and get back to her parents and the land she loved, she'd pushed hard, studied harder and didn't have much of a life outside of her textbooks and labs. Near the end of her first year at Johns Hopkins, Claire received a call from her grandmother, breaking the news her parents had been killed in a plane crash.

"How old were you when they passed?"

"I was in medical school." The shock of that call reverberated through her as if it was only yesterday.

The news hit right before a huge exam. For the first time in her life, she'd been too stymied by grief to study effectively. She blew the exam and nearly dropped out of medical school. After a talk with her advisor, she'd pulled herself together, finished her studies and interned at a hospital in New York City. "As soon as I had my license to practice medicine, I joined Doctors Without Borders and returned to the African continent."

Irish lifted her hand. "I'm glad you did," he said softly. "If you hadn't, I'd be a dead man today."

She squeezed his fingers. "Then it's a good thing I happened to see you fall out of a helicopter."

"Dr. Boyette," a deep male voice called out from the other side of the tent flap.

Claire gasped and spun toward the entrance. "I'll be right out, Dr. Jamo."

"Do you have someone in your tent? I hear voices."

"No, no. I was just talking to myself," she called out, hating lying to her friend and colleague, but he was better off not knowing about her guest. If she could make it through the day without revealing he was there, she'd get him out that night before the refugees and the rebels were any wiser.

Where he'd go, she wasn't sure. The man was a SEAL, he was bound to have resources who could get him out of the area.

Part of her wanted to go with him, to leave the danger behind. The other part of her knew he was heading into danger and might not make it out alive. And she wanted him to live.

Claire pressed a finger to her lips and nodded toward the pallet.

Irish slipped into the sleeping area and ducked beneath the cot, completely out of sight before Claire opened the tent flap.

Dr. Jamo stepped inside and closed the flap behind him. "You have someone in here," her colleague said.

Claire stepped backward. "Why do you say that?" she asked.

"I heard you talking to him. Is it one of the men from the helicopter crash last night?"

Claire shook her head, her face heating. Then she nodded, unable to lie to someone she respected as much as Dr. Jamo. "Yes."

Dr. Jamo's eyes widened as he stared toward the stack of boxes. "Where is he?"

Claire tilted her head toward the sleeping area.

"He cannot stay," Dr. Jamo said. "You put our people at risk by bringing this man among them."

Claire nodded.

Irish stood, rising above the boxes.

"I'll leave as soon as it gets dark outside."

Dr. Jamo's gaze swept over the tall man. "What happened to him?"

"He fell from a helicopter." Claire gave him a breakdown of Irish's injuries and concussion. "I'd rather he stayed longer, but I realize it's not safe. No one else knows he's here but you and me."

Dr. Jamo frowned. "American?"

Irish nodded. "Born and raised in Texas. My mother was Irish, my father was Texan."

Dr. Jamo paced away from Claire and her charge. "If Umar finds him among us, he will take him and use this American as an example to all other Americans who venture onto Somali soil. Then he'll kill every one of the people of Samada as a warning not to harbor foreign infidels."

"I know."

"And yet, you still brought him among us?" Dr. Jamo waved his hand toward the tent's exit, behind which the women and children of Samada lived in tents, slept on the ground and starved for food. Thin from malnutrition, they were tired and dispirited already from being displaced from their homes into a makeshift refugee camp. Now they were frightened from sounds of gunfire and last night's crash.

Guilt washed over Claire when she

considered their lives and what it meant to introduce more danger to them with the American's presence. Still, she couldn't have left Irish to die in the rubble, or to be discovered and tortured by al-Shabaab.

"I promise to get him out of here tonight. In the meantime, we'll keep quiet and ensure no one else finds out he's here."

"It is a small camp," Dr. Jamo reminded her. "Everyone knows everyone else's business."

She stiffened her back. "Then I'll just have to be doubly careful. As it is, we can't move him now without everyone seeing him, including whatever rebels might be lurking nearby."

Dr. Jamo gave Irish a narrow-eyed glare. "It isn't safe."

"Agreed.☐" Irish nodded. "I'll be gone tonight."

The native doctor stared long and hard at Irish and then turned to Claire. "Nahabo needs our assistance. Her baby is coming."

Claire shot a glance at Irish. "You'll be okay today?"

He nodded. "Go. I'll be as quiet as a mouse."

"This might take a while. No birth is every quite the same." She gave him a weak smile then pushed through the tent flap and out into the open, followed by her colleague.

Dr. Jamo gripped her elbow. "Tonight."

The intensity of that one word hit Claire square in the gut. "I promise."

The rest of the day was spent delivering Nahabo's baby, treating children for infections and checking on those too sick to leave the hospital tent.

Near the end of the day, a dozen black men with rifles stormed into camp.

The women grabbed their children. Those on the edge of camp slipped into the trees and brush. Those caught in the middle gathered their children close.

Rebel fighters split in two groups, each taking a different side of the camp. Using the barrel of their rifles, they jerked aside the tent flaps to reveal the occupants inside. So far they hadn't made it to hers. But it wouldn't be long.

Dr. Jamo had gone with a man to check on a shepherd outside the camp. Claire had been treating a young girl for a nasty cut on her leg that was infected.

Though her heart hammered against her ribs, Claire refused to reveal to the rebels she was rattled by their abrupt entrance and afraid they'd find Irish. She continued to clean and dress the wound until the task was finished.

"You!" The leader of the band of rebels pointed his rifle at Claire. "Come."

She set the child on the ground and gave her a gentle push toward her mother. Then Claire stood. "Where are we going?"

He nodded toward the hospital tent. "Medicine."

"Those are sick people."

A fierce frown settled across his forehead. He rattled off something to one of the women, who broke down and cried. He backhanded her, sending her skidding across the packed dirt.

"Hey!" Claire glared at the man and bent to help the woman to her feet. "I'll go with you. Just leave these people alone."

Shuffling feet and rattling weapon harnesses alerted Claire to Dr. Jamo's entrance into the camp. He held up his hands and bowed his head, a clear sign of submission. They didn't want any trouble. Jamo spoke in short, crisp words to the leader.

The ink-black man with the big rifle snorted and nodded toward Claire.

"He wants you to take your medicine. Umar is injured and requires our assistance." Dr. Jamo's lips tightened briefly. "I offered to go instead, but he wants you."

"Will they bring me back?" she asked,

her stomach tight with worry for Irish.

"They say they will." Dr. Jamo touched her arm. "They have to be kind to you since you will be working on Umar."

"And if I work on the leader, and he dies?" she finished in a whisper, her gaze not on Dr. Jamo but the team leader and his scary gun.

"You have to make certain he does not die." Dr. Jamo turned toward the rebel leader, saying beneath his breath. "Your first challenge will be getting to your medicine without exposing our guest."

Claire forced a smile. "Tell them I'll be right back with my medicine bag." She turned toward her tent.

Dr. Jamo translated.

Their leader wasn't letting her out of his sight, following her all the way to the tent.

Claire paused with her hand on the tent flap. Damn. If the rebel entered the tent, he might snoop around and discover the American. "Wait here," she said and slipped through the entrance.

Her rebel shadow entered behind her.

Heart pounding, hands clenched, muscles bunched and ready to run, she stared around the interior, her focus zooming in on the floor pallet. The blankets and sleeping bag had been transferred to the cot. Irish and all of his gear were gone.

Letting go of the breath she'd held, Claire hurried to collect her bag, stocking it with additional penicillin, gauze, tape and rubbing alcohol. She figured, after last night's battle, more than Umar would be needing medical attention.

When she stepped out into the open, the rebel leader grabbed the tent fabric and yanked hard. Some of the poles snapped and the tent collapsed to the ground, leaving lumps beneath. As if that wasn't good enough, he aimed his weapon at the tent and fired a burst of bullets at the lumps.

Claire winced, praying Irish really had escaped the tent and that he wasn't hiding in one of the boxes. Not that his big frame would fit in them. Not knowing where he was, all she could do was hope he'd find his way back to his team.

Meanwhile, she had her own worries. The fact they'd destroyed her tent meant one thing. She was not to return.

Moments later, the rebels smashed, kicked, tore and demolished the refugee camp. Women wailed and shielded their babies from the attack, only to take the brunt of abuse.

Claire stepped forward. "Stop. You

don't have to do this. I'm going with you. Please," she begged. "Leave these people alone."

At the edge of the refugee compound, Dr. Jamo stood with his hands secured behind his back with a length of rope, his lips tight, anger burning in his eyes.

"They're taking you, too?" Claire asked. A hard shove from behind sent her sprawling in the dirt, her bag sliding out in front of her.

"Seems they want both of us to patch up those injured in last night's raid."

"Someone needs to stay and help these people rebuild or relocate." Claire's heart ached for the damage with which the refugees had to contend.

"They won't listen." He turned his face so that she could see where he'd been hit in the temple. A trail of blood dried on his dark skin.

Herded like animals, Claire and Dr. Jamo trudged through the bush back to Samada.

Claire hated seeing all the destruction in the small village. The main building of mud, sticks and grass had been leveled. Many of the smaller huts were intact, but some had been burned to the ground, the stench of smoldering grass filled the air.

The rebel team leader shoved her

toward one of the grass huts, and she ducked inside.

Lying on a mat on the floor was a large black man with deep black eyes and shrapnel imbedded in his leg, abdomen and arms. His gaze shot to her, his eyes narrowing.

"You will fix me," he said in English.

"I'll do what I can." Claire knelt on one side of Umar.

Dr. Jamo was pushed to his knees on the other side.

"Fix me or you die." Umar lifted a pistol in his bloody hand and pointed it at Claire's head.

Nothing like a little incentive to make her job easier. She prayed she could fix what was wrong with the man. He looked like he'd been run through a shredder.

Claire removed scissors from her bag and cut the pant leg all the way up to his thigh to expose the jagged piece of metal jutting from his skin. It hadn't hit a main artery, or the man already would be dead.

Dr. Jamo cut away the man's shirt to get a better look at the shrapnel embedded in his chest.

Between the two of them and several bright, battery powered lanterns, they worked pulling out shrapnel and stitching the open wounds. Umar refused sedatives, preferring to remain awake and as alert as possible. When they'd addressed most of what they could find, Claire and Dr. Jamo sat back. Now his recovery was up to antibiotics and Umar's system to fight off infection. After all the people the al-Shabaab leader had murdered, Claire found it difficult to help him. But to refuse to treat a sick or injured human wasn't in her nature or her Hippocratic oath.

The al-Shabaab emir waved them away with a few curt words in Arabic.

"He wants to rest," Dr. Jamo said.

As she left the well-lit hut, Claire realized daylight had turned to darkness, reminding her of the original plan for Irish to leave the refugee compound after sunset. She wondered if any of the refugees had seen him slip out of the camp, and if they'd tell the rebels they'd seen him.

Claire hoped not. She wished him well and hoped he made it back safely to his team. Now that she and Dr. Jamo had patched up the boss, they were led to the center of town where other men lay in various degrees of pain and dismemberment from shrapnel and bullet wounds.

She and her colleague worked long into the night helping those they could and declaring those who'd passed. Around three in the morning, beyond exhaustion, Claire stood and pressed her hands to the small of her back.

A guard nudged her with the barrel of his weapon, indicating she should follow him to a nearby hut.

Dr. Jamo made to follow, but another guard spoke curtly to him and pointed his weapon at the doctor's chest.

"What's he saying?" Claire asked as she was forced to move away.

"He does not want us to be together."

"Will you be all right?" Claire called out.

"I'm not worried about me. I'm more worried about you," Dr. Jamo spoke angrily to the guard holding him back.

The guard spit at his feet and slammed the butt of his weapon into Dr. Jamo's gut.

The older man doubled over.

"Dr. Jamo!" Claire cried out.

Her guard shoved her through a door.

She turned immediately and fought to get out.

A fairly new white Land Rover, with a green logo of a dove in flight painted on the side, drove into the village center. The driver climbed out and opened the back passenger door.

Dr. Jamo was shoved into the back seat.

"Dr. Jamo!" Claire clawed at the guard, trying to push him out of the way to get to Dr. Jamo.

The doors closed on Dr. Jamo, and the Land Rover hesitated only a minute before it sped north out of the village.

The flimsy stick door to the hut shut in her face, and Claire collapsed to the floor, tears welling in her eyes. Where were they taking Dr. Jamo, and what did they have planned for her?

Chapter Four

AT THE FIRST SIGN of trouble, Irish had gathered his equipment and slipped out the back of the tent. Dr. Boyette would be in a great deal of trouble if the rebels found one of last night's attackers hidden in her tent. The residents of the refugee camp had been too concerned about the rebels to glance his way. He made it into the relative concealment of the bushes and trees surrounding the camp.

His first instinct and his training was to find his way back to Djibouti where he hoped to meet up with his team. If they had escaped the crash site before the rebels got there, they would head north. But Irish stuck around, staying out of sight, watching to see what the rebels had in mind for Claire and the refugees.

When the rebels urged her and Dr. Jamo at gunpoint to return to Samada, Irish couldn't, in good conscience, leave until he knew Claire would be all right. He needed to get back to his team, but he wanted to settle things with Claire. After all, the woman had put herself at risk to save his life. Following at a safe distance, he arrived on the edge of Samada.

Security was lax, many of the rebels having been injured in the attack. Apparently, no one thought they would receive a repeat attack that soon.

That kind of attitude was in Irish's favor, if action was required to free Claire and her colleague.

Claire and Dr. Jamo had been led to a small hut near the center of the village. They disappeared into the hut and stayed for nearly four hours. Several of Umar's men entered and left, but Claire and Dr. Jamo remained inside.

If Irish had to bet, he would say Umar was injured in the attack and needed medical attention. A lot of medical attention, based on the amount of time they were taking to come back out.

The sun set on the village and darkness crept in with the incessant sound of insects chirping. Finally, the door to the hut opened. Claire and Dr. Jamo were escorted out and split up.

Not good. Being a woman, Claire wasn't safe with any of the rebels. She cried out to Dr. Jamo, but the rebels shoved him into a vehicle and sped away. Dr. Boyette was taken to another hut closer to the edge of the village.

If Irish played his cards right, he could sneak up to the hut, dispatch the guard and get Claire out. He waited, hoping the guard would exit. When he didn't, Irish made his move, inching closer to the village.

He had spied one sentry on his side of the village. The man's face had been cut severely, and the wound had been roughly patched with gauze and tape. He looked like hell, and probably felt like it, having to stand guard duty with a damaged face and probably a splitting headache.

Irish slipped up beside the sentry and slit his throat. He crumpled to the ground with no more than a sigh. Irish waited outside the hut, listening for the guard to exit. Instead, he heard a grunt and Claire's voice. "Get the hell off me, you bastard! If Umar finds out you've messed with his doctor, he'll kill you." A loud crack, like someone slapped another person, sent Irish through the door and into the grass hut.

In the light beam from a flashlight lying on the floor, Irish saw the rebel guard had pinned Claire to the ground and he tore at her trousers.

She rocked beneath him, a bright red handprint on her cheek, her jaw set in a grim line. With all the force she could muster in such close proximity, she jerked up her knee, slamming it into the man's groin.

Irish grabbed the man from behind, stuck his knife in his jugular and shoved him to the side. Then he reached out to Claire. "Let's get out of here."

"I thought you were gone," she whispered.

"I couldn't leave until I knew you were safe. I owe you."

"You don't owe me anything."

Irish eased open the door and peered through the crack. A group of five rebel fighters were headed toward the hut.

"Can't go that way." He closed the door made of sticks and twine, and secured it closed with a piece of cording. Irish stepped to the opposite side of the hut and jammed his knife through the stick walls, slicing through the grass twine holding the sticks together. He kicked an opening, looked through to ensure no one was lurking on the other side. Then he grabbed the dead guard's gun and ammo, turned back to Claire and said, "Let's go."

She held back. "I can't. They took Dr. Jamo. What if they bring him back? I can't leave without knowing he's safe."

"I seriously doubt he'll be coming back." Irish glanced toward the door of the hut. "But five burly men, who look like they mean business, are headed toward this hut. We can't stay here with two of their dead buddies."

Claire nodded, grabbed her doctor's bag and stepped over the body of the man who'd tried to assault her. "You're right, let's go."

Irish was first through the opening. He checked left and right before handing Claire through the hole. Then he pushed the sticks back in place as the door to the hut rattled on the other side.

Things were about to get hot in the village. "Run." Grabbing her hand, he raced for the bushes bordering the village, half-dragging Claire along. She dug her heels into the ground, pulling him to a stop. "That's my vehicle." She pointed to a beat-up old Land Rover standing beside a hut. She jerked her hand from his and ran toward it.

"What the hell, Claire?" He ran after her, certain bullets would be cutting them down at any moment.

What were the chances the keys were in it?

The rebels would be forcing open the door to the hut about now and find the dead guard lying on the floor. Irish hoped they wouldn't expect whoever killed the guard to stay in the village.

Claire tossed her bag into the back seat, slid into the driver's seat and bent low, her hand sliding beneath the seat. "I kept the spare key under the seat. I doubt they would have found it."

"If you want to live to tell your children this story, you'd better find it."

Her search ended, and she held up a key.

"Great. Scoot and stay down."

Claire slid across to the passenger seat and hunkered low.

Irish tossed the rifle into Claire's lap and slid the key into the ignition.

A shout rose up from the hut they'd left.

"Time to punch out." He turned the key and the engine coughed, turned over and died.

"The motor can be cantankerous, but it will start eventually," Claire said.

Great. He hoped it started before the rebels discovered them in it and peppered them with bullets. Turning the key a second time, he heard the engine turn over and rumble to life.

Irish yanked the shift into gear and slammed down his foot on the accelerator. The Land Rover shot out from the side of the village into the woods.

A bullet blew out the back window, scattering glass throughout the vehicle.

Crashing through the brush, Irish yanked the steering wheel to the right in time to miss hitting a tree.

Claire slammed against the passenger door and held on to the armrest. "Turn right here!" she shouted.

Bracing himself, he swung right, and the Land Rover bumped out onto the dirt road leading into the village. It wouldn't take long for the rebel fighters to catch up to them. Irish glanced at the gas gauge. They had half a tank of fuel. If he could put some distance between them and the rebels, they had a chance of making it all the way to Djibouti. Pushing the vehicle as fast as it would go, he raced down the road, lights out, guided only by the moon and sparing on the brakes to avoid giving their pursuers lights to aim at.

Claire turned halfway around in her seat, looking out the back, shattered window. "Three vehicles are following. No. Make it four."

"We may have to turn off the main road and ditch it in the bushes." He didn't like being out in the open. But then the rebels didn't have helicopters. He and Claire only had to evade the rebels and make it across the border into Djibouti.

"They're gaining on us."

Irish pushed the Land Rover faster. They rounded a bend in the road, going so fast, the vehicle tipped, the tires slid and they nearly toppled over. Removing his foot from the accelerator for only a moment brought the SUV back to earth. As soon as they hit another straight stretch, he goosed it.

"They're in the curve," Claire shouted.

A glance in the rearview mirror confirmed. Headlights shined into Irish's eyes for a brief second, tilted, then tumbled to the left. That vehicle had rolled.

One down. Three still following them, but they'd slowed to take the curve, giving Irish a few seconds more of a lead. It wasn't enough. The old Land Rover just didn't have the speed it needed. They'd have to find a place to hide until the rebels gave up and moved on.

When he came to a fork in the dirt road, Irish slowed by easing off the accelerator.

"Which way?" Claire asked.

"The direction they will least expect." He took the more-traveled road, headed north toward Djibouti.

"Won't they expect you to take the more-traveled road?"

He nodded. "Yes, but they won't expect this." Removing his foot from the accelerator, he let the vehicle slow without applying the brakes, and then he swerved off the road, zigzagged through the trees for several hundred feet before coming

61

out on the other road. "The problem with dirt roads is they leave a cloud of dust until it settles. Hopefully, they won't realize we left the road until they are farther along. By then, we'll be long gone."

"And if they split up at the fork?" Claire asked.

"They'll be closer, but we only have to contend with one or two trucks full of angry rebels, not three." Irish glanced in her direction. The moonlight bathed Claire's face in pale blue light. His angel.

"Sounds like a gamble any way you look at it," she said.

He dragged his gaze back to the road ahead, shooting a glance in the rearview mirror through the shattered back window. "Maybe, but it's what we have to work with, unless you prefer to ditch the vehicle and go on foot?"

Shaking her head, she held up her hands, her teeth flashing in a grin. "No, thank you. I'll take my chances on wheels."

"Good, because we have a tail again." Irish focused on the road ahead.

Claire turned in her seat, watching the road behind them. "Only one set of headlights."

"Good."

"Do you think they can see us?"

"With the moon so bright, they might. But then they'd have to turn off their headlights and let their eyes adjust to the moonlight. We might have the edge."

"They have the faster vehicle," Claire said, her voice low, intense.

Another fork in the road presented itself. This time, the road to the left was the one less traveled. It appeared to be more of a washed-out track than an actual road. Slowing enough to enter the trail without stirring up too much dust, Irish eased onto the track and around a curve, praying the other rebel's vehicle was far enough behind that the haze of dust would settle before they reached the fork.

"If we head far enough west, we will cross into Ethiopia," Claire said. "In Samada, we were only about twenty miles east of the border crossing."

"From what we learned about Umar, he doesn't care about borders. He and his men go where they want to go, kill whomever they want to kill."

Claire stared at the road behind them. "That's not reassuring."

"All the more reason to lose our tail for good." The Land Rover bumped along the trail, moving slowly over the rutted road.

Fifteen minutes passed, and no headlights appeared behind them.

"I don't see any lights," Claire said. "Think we lost them?"

"I hope so." Irish settled into as steady a pace as he could maintain on the ruined road. "We'll keep going until we run out of road, or get too sleepy to keep going."

"Where are we aiming for?"

"Djibouti, where I can meet up with my team. I hope they made it back." If not, he'd be right back in Somalia looking for them in a recovery operation.

"Can your team help find Dr. Jamo?"

"I'll work with my team leader to make that happen."

"If you can't help," Claire said, "I'll find someone who can."

Irish shot a glance her way. If the hard set of her jaw was any indication of her determination, he'd have to do a lot of fancy talking to convince her otherwise, or get buy-in from his SEAL team to mount a rescue operation for the kidnapped Somali doctor.

Claire must have fallen asleep. A big bump slammed her head against the window, waking her.

"Sorry. I didn't see that one. Must be getting tired."

She looked through the window but saw only scrub brush. "You should let me drive for a while."

"No, I think it's safe to say we lost them for the time being. It's getting close to daylight. If I'm not mistaken, we're back in Somalia on one of the less-traveled roads. We should find a place to hide and sleep for a couple hours during the daylight and then push north to the border of Djibouti."

"I take it you don't have a passport with you."

Irish grinned. "Not something SEALs carry on a mission."

"I have mine, if we need it. But how will we make it past the checkpoints, if you don't have yours?"

"We won't need them if we stay off the main roads and travel mostly at night. Once we near the border, you can drop me off. I'll cross on foot."

She nodded, scanning the road ahead for any possibilities of hiding places as the path wound through the hills. The moon had made its way into the western sky, sinking low and giving little light to navigate by.

Irish still drove with the headlights off to keep from being spotted by rebels or soldiers at checkpoints. The farther north they moved, the drier the terrain became and the more rugged. If they didn't find a place to hide the Land Rover soon, daylight would be upon them, and they'd be fair game for anything from truckloads of rebels to Somali military.

As they passed through a narrow pass between hills, Claire spotted a copse of low trees and bushes a hundred yards off the road. The foliage was of sufficient size to conceal the Land Rover. She pointed. "Do you see that?"

Irish nodded, drove the Land Rover off the road and eased it into the brush. Once the back end of the vehicle was completely surrounded by trees and bushes, he turned off the engine.

"Might as well get comfortable. We'll sleep here until the temp gets too hot. Then we'll take our chances on the road. If we can get close enough to one of the larger cities, we can blend in with the traffic." Irish slipped down out of the vehicle and rounded to the back where he opened the rear door.

Claire climbed out of the passenger side, stretched and walked to the rear of the SUV.

Irish pointed at the interior floorboard. "There's enough room for you to lie down and get some real rest back here."

The rear seats of the vehicle had been removed long ago to make room for cargo, which had suited Claire just fine for her trip into the remote regions of Somalia. Though she'd fallen asleep on the journey, she hadn't slept for more than ten minutes at a time.

Irish, on the other hand, had suffered a concussion and he'd yet to sleep as well. He'd done all the driving over rough terrain and had to be exhausted.

Claire shook her head. "You take the first shift of sleep. I'll stand guard. You've been injured."

Irish braced his hands on his hips. "You need to sleep, as well. Look, we can both lie down. At least we'll be rested when we have to get going later."

Claire stared at the interior and then at Irish.

He grinned. "I promise not to touch you unless you ask. Hell, I can sleep on the ground if that will make you feel safer."

"No, you don't have to do that. I'm sure we can share the space. Although it will be tight." She climbed up into the back of the vehicle and reached for her doctor bag. "I have a couple of bottles of water and some granola bars." She handed him a bottle and a bar. "It's not much, but enough to keep up our energy for a little longer." The smile he gave her warmed her insides.

"You're amazing." Irish accepted her

offering.

She snorted softly. "Not as though it was a fine dining experience."

"When you're dry and hungry, they're heaven." He opened the bottle and downed a quarter of the liquid before he tipped it up. "We need to ration in case we have to hike our way out of Somalia."

Nodding, she drank from her bottle. "How far do you think we are from the Djibouti border?"

"I'm betting about five to six hours."

"Doesn't sound like much."

"It is when you have to drive in lights-out conditions and through potentially hostile situations." He rubbed a hand on his neck.

"Once we get to the more urban areas, shouldn't we be all right?"

"As long as Umar's al-Shabaab rebels aren't controlling the checkpoints and border crossings."

"Does he have that kind of influence?"

"We might find out sooner than we'd like." He ate half the bar and folded the wrapper around it.

Claire followed suit and stored the bottles and remaining granola bars in her bag. Then she stretched out on the hard floor of the Land Rover and tried to get comfortable. "I think the ground might actually be softer."

"Come here." Irish laid back and pulled her into the crook of his arm. "I've been known to make a great pillow."

She stiffened at first, afraid to relax with him so close. Her pulse jumped with each breath he took. "One of your many girlfriends told you that?" she quipped, trying to ease the tension apparently only she felt.

He chuckled. "At least half a dozen of them."

The sound of his voice rumbled against her ear. With nowhere else to put her hand, she rested it on his chest, the hard muscles surprisingly reassuring at her fingertips.

His hold tightened around her, bringing her body against his. "Better?"

"Umm." Better than she could have imagined. He smelled of dust, male musk and the outdoors, a purely masculine scent that set her insides into turmoil. She'd had lovers in college, but none that lasted. During her internal medicine residency at Johns Hopkins, she'd had an affair with one of the other interns.

"You're still so tense. Do I make you nervous?" His other hand reached out to brush a loose strand of hair from her face. "I promise, I don't bite." Then he kissed her forehead.

Claire's heart rate rocketed. "Why did you do that?"

"You still seemed scared, and well...I've been wanting to do that since the last time I kissed you."

"And you promised you wouldn't do it again."

"I lied." He kissed her forehead again. "So sue me."

His warm breath and the words spoken in a low, bone-melting whisper, made Claire's nervous tension dissolve to be replaced by an entirely different kind of tension seeping through her system with every beat of her heart.

Her fingers slid across his shirt. She wanted them to slide across his skin.

"Ach, lass, you'll be wearin' a hole in me shirt before ya know it," he said with his delightful, over-exaggerated Irish accent. Lifting her hand, he pressed his lips to her fingers and laid her hand across his raspy chin. Then he shucked his shirt, dragging it over his shoulders and off his body.

Claire cupped his cheek, loving the rough feel of his two-day-old beard. She reached up and ran her fingers over his closely cropped hair. "How's your head today?"

"Never clearer," he said, his hands releasing the last button on her shirt.

Feeling bolder by the minute, the continued contact with his body heating her core, she ran her hand down his face, tracing his lips and the hard line of his chin. Moving lower, she skimmed his muscled neck and traced his collarbone, finally arriving at the broad expanse of his naked chest. She's seen it before when she'd checked him for injuries. But this time, he was awake, he wasn't her patient, and he was so very conscious and participating in her exploration.

Irish's finger curled beneath her chin and lifted, urging her gaze to meet his. "I didn't suggest we rest here to take advantage of a pretty lady."

"Oh? I thought that was your plan all along. Blow up an al-Shabaab leader, rescue a lady doctor and ravage her on the run from an angry terrorist. Does that scenario work for you..."

He bent and captured her words before she could finish her nervous jabber. The kiss took her breath away, making her forget they were in the back of an SUV, in danger of discovery and ultimately death.

Claire's entire focus was on the man holding her, possessing her lips and cradling her against his body in such a way that made her want more than a kiss, more than to feel his chest beneath her

71

hand. She reached lower, skimming the hardened plains of his abdomen, crossing to the waistband of his black trousers, held securely in place by an equally black belt.

She fumbled with the buckle until, once again, he brushed aside her fingers.

"Are you sure you want to do this?" he asked.

"Aren't you?" Claire glanced up at him in the moonlight edging through the side window, suddenly unsure of his intentions and her own ability to inspire passion.

"Darlin', I've wanted to do this since I laid eyes on my angel." He slipped his arm from beneath her neck and came up on his elbow. "I've never wanted someone as badly."

"Even if it's in a foreign country in the back of an SUV? After being injured?" her voice faded at the intensity in his eyes.

"Yes. Even in the back of an SUV, like teenagers on their first date."

Tingles of excitement spread throughout her body. Irish wanted her. A surge of power emboldened Claire to gently cup the back of his neck and drag his mouth down to hers.

He claimed her, his tongue pushed past her lips, slipped between her teeth and caressed hers in a long, slow glide. He tasted of granola and kissed like nobody's business.

Claire curled into him, her leg sliding along his calf, and up his thigh. She couldn't get close enough, and the clothes between them frustrated her.

When he finally came up for air, he trailed feather-soft kisses along her chin to her earlobe and down to the crazily beating pulse at the base of her neck. As his lips left her skin, Irish pulled her to a sitting position, snagged the opening of her shirt, and dragged it off her shoulders and arms, tossing it over the seat. Then he circled his hands behind her and unclipped her bra, sliding the straps slowly over her shoulders and down her arms, letting her breasts spill out.

For a moment, he sat back and stared, and then reached out to touch the peaked nipples. "You're beautiful."

She should have been shy, covering her breasts with her arms, but the hungry look in Irish's eyes only spurred Claire to be more brazen. Her fingers found the button on her trousers and flipped it free.

Before she could unzip them, Irish took over, sliding down the zipper, his fingers slipping beneath the fabric into her panties to cover her sex.

Claire closed her eyes, her breathing coming in short, ragged gulps. She wanted him to feel the warmth and wetness he inspired. More than that, she wanted to be naked with him. She shoved the trousers over her hips and, with his help, pulled them off her legs. The cool metal bed of the vehicle felt good against her burning skin. Then she reached for the button on his pants. With surgical accuracy, she flipped open the button and dragged down his zipper. His cock surged free, filling her hand, long, hard and thick.

"Oh, darlin', I'm trying to take it slow, but you're making me crazy."

"Then don't hold back." Her fingers curled around him and squeezed, pulling him toward her. "I'm as hot for you as you are for me." Shocked by the words coming out of her own mouth, she couldn't take them back and didn't want to. She'd started down this path and couldn't wait to get to the finish line.

"You don't know how badly I want you."

She chuckled, feeling more confident and secure in her desirability. "I have an idea."

"I don't have protection. It's not something I carry on an operation."

Stilling her movements, she frowned. "Are you clean?"

"No STDs."

"I'm on the pill, and they're in my

satchel." She tilted her head. "Any more objections?"

"No." Irish dropped down to capture one of her breasts between his lips and sucked it into his mouth. He swirled his tongue around the nipple and nibbled on the tightening bud. Then he shifted to her other breast and performed the same ministrations. His fingers trailed across her ribs, moving south to the triangle of hair over her mons. Slipping a finger between her folds, he stroked that tiny strip of flesh packed with enough nerve endings to shoot fiery sensations throughout her body.

Claire raised her hips, wanting more. Her hand convulsed around his cock, and she dragged him closer.

"Not yet," he whispered, his finger continuing to stroke her there. He dipped into the dampness of her channel and traced a line of the thick lubricant up to her clit, swirling around the nubbin.

An instant later, she launched over the edge in a burst of fireworks shooting from her core outward to the very tips of her fingers and toes.

Irish settled between her legs, pressing the thick head of his staff against her moist opening, easing in a little at a time.

Impatient to have it all, Claire

wrapped her legs around his waist, dug her heels into his ass and took him into her.

He thrust inside, filling her, stretching her deliciously.

She dropped her heels to the metal bed of the SUV and pushed up, taking all of him.

Settling into a rhythm, he moved in and out of her body, the friction sending her back up the incline to her second orgasm of the early morning.

He thrust one last time, burying himself deep inside her, his cock throbbing against the walls of her channel.

To hold him there, she dug her fingers into his buttocks until the intensity of their union eased.

Then he collapsed on the floor of the SUV beside her, rolling her into his arms, nuzzling her neck with his lips. "That was insane," he said.

She smiled, lying back on a hard metal floor, not caring that it dug into her backside. "It was, wasn't it?" Never had she felt as beautifully replete as she did at that moment. Surrounded by the desert hills of Somalia, with the sun cresting over the horizon and cradled in the arms of a handsome, virile man, Claire could forget for a moment they were in danger and being hunted by al-Shabaab fighters.

Chapter Five

IRISH SLEPT for a few hours with Claire nestled against his side, her body warm, her curves fitting perfectly with his harder plains. He would have lain there all day had the sun not become too hot. They'd have to get on the move or be cooked inside the Land Rover.

Pressing a light kiss to Claire's forehead, Irish woke the pretty doctor. "Hey, beautiful."

She blinked several times and then stared up at him with those blue-gray eyes. "Morning already?"

"Halfway through the day and it's going to be a hot one." He slapped her bare ass and squeezed it. "As much as I'd like a repeat performance, we'd better get moving."

"Umm. I want a rain check on the repeat performance." She sat up and pushed her long, straight blond hair out of her face, her breasts bobbing with the movement.

"You're on." Irish couldn't resist the temptation and bent to capture one rosy nipple in his mouth, sucking gently on the tip before letting go with a sigh.

"Preferably in a nice soft bed."

They gathered their clothing, dressed, ate the last of the granola bars and drank half of the water left in the bottles. The day would be a long one of traveling backcountry.

On the road again, Irish drove north. Without a map, he did the best he could. With the sun angling toward its zenith, he wasn't always sure he was headed in the right direction. He only hoped their fuel would last long enough to get them back to a town with a gas station.

After driving a little over an hour, Irish noticed a flock of birds circling in the sky ahead.

"What are those?" Claire leaned forward. "Buzzards?"

Irish squinted in the bright sun, wishing he had his sunglasses. "Appear to be."

"But there are so many." Staring ahead, she frowned. "That's a village." Her voice sounded strained.

Irish slowed the vehicle as they neared the traditional mud and stick buildings with their grass roofs. The birds dipped down and rose up from a point ahead.

"I don't see any people moving about," Claire said. "No women or children. Like the village is deserted."

78

As they passed between the first of the structures, Irish could see why. Or more to the point, he could smell why.

Bodies lay in the dirt, near the doorways, inside their homes and in the road. Bloated, picked over by the scavengers. Dead.

"Stop the car," Claire demanded.

Irish did, but before Claire could open the door and jump out, he grabbed her arm. "Are you sure you want to get out? What if they have some disease that wiped them out? Are you willing to risk your life?"

Claire bit her lip, her fingers gripping the door handle. "I can't just ignore this."

Irish understood her desire to help, but these people were beyond help. "You have to. You don't have the HAZMAT equipment to move among them. If they have a communicable disease, they could contaminate you and then you'd spread it to the next place we stop." He pressed his foot on the accelerator, sending the Land Rover through the village and out the other side, dodging dead bodies.

Claire closed her eyes and nodded. "You're right. There was nothing we could do, but drive on and report this to the CDC. They will escalate. If the country wants help, they will send out people."

"And they will be better prepared."

Irish increased their speed, putting as much distance between them and the stench of death, the haunting images of people lying in the dirt, mothers holding babies with their eyes turned skyward, lifeless.

The road ultimately connected to another, sending them into a small town. There, Irish bartered the spare tire for fuel for the vehicle, keeping a close watch on the road in and out, ready to make a run for it, should trouble catch up to them. When he was finished at the pump, he climbed in and shifted into gear. "There's a store a block from here. We can get food and water."

Irish parked in back of the rundown building that barely looked habitable. "Much as I love it, your blond hair will draw attention."

"I'll stay here and keep a low profile."

He nodded. "Along with the low profile, keep your eyes open for any men carrying guns."

With a serious expression, Claire saluted and ruined it with a grin. "Yes, sir."

He shook his head, leaned across to kiss her and climbed out of the SUV. "I'll hurry."

As soon as he entered the small store and couldn't see Claire anymore, Irish's

ELLE JAMES

gut clenched.

Far enough away from the al-Shabaab
fighters, he felt certain they would be
relatively safe, but they'd left an angry
Umar nursing his wounds. Based on
intelligence, the man carried a grudge and
wielded a pretty big stick that extended
across the small country of Somalia, as
well as into Ethiopia. The sooner they
made it into Djibouti, the better. He
spoke briefly to the storeowner, learning
the border was closer than he'd thought,
within an hour's drive.

Somewhat relieved, he made his
purchases of bottled water and uncut
fruit. He threw in a colorful shash, a
headscarf Somali and Ethiopian women
wore over their heads, and a plain brown
kaftan. After paying for the items, he
stepped out of the store and rounded to
the back.

At first glance, he didn't see Claire in
the passenger seat. His heart skipped
several beats until he remembered she'd
said she'd keep a low profile. Picking up
the pace, he crossed to the vehicle and
peered in the window.

The passenger seat was empty.

Irish tossed his purchases into the
back, and stared around the parking area
and street beyond. Where had Claire
gone? His heart thumping against his

81

chest, he moved past the vehicle and ran to the edge of the building.

He found her there, crouched in the bushes, looking beyond to the main road passing through the little hamlet. Dropping to his haunches beside her, he stared through a gap between the branches. "What're you doing here?"

She nodded toward the street where a truck pulled to a stop and eight armed black men climbed down and scattered in different directions.

He grabbed her hand. "Time to go."

They raced back to the Land Rover and climbed inside.

Irish eased out onto a secondary street, hoping to bypass the men carrying the guns. He traveled several blocks and ultimately pulled behind the ruins of a building. The only way out of the small town was on the main road headed north. Staying put wouldn't be an option, either. If the men searched hard enough, they'd find the Land Rover.

"For safety's sake, let's get away from this vehicle," Irish said.

Claire nodded. "Do you think they're looking for us?"

"They could be. The owner of the gas station saw us and so did the guy at the market. Anyone else might point out where we've been and which way we were headed." He reached into the back where he'd stowed the purchased clothes and handed them to Claire. "Put these on."

She studied the kaftan and scarf and quickly pulled them over her clothing and hair, wrapping the ends of the scarf around her face, hiding as much of her hair and pale skin as possible. "What about you?"

"I'll stick to the shadows." He removed his military gear from the back of the vehicle, stashed it beneath the crumbled masonry, and then he pulled the bolt out of the weapon he'd taken from the Somali rebel, rendering it useless.

Claire stuffed the water and food into her doctor bag and slipped it over her arm. It wasn't in keeping with her outfit, but they didn't have time to worry about that fact.

"Stay here for a minute." Irish slipped away, hugging the shadows, heading back toward the truck and the gunmen. He stopped a block short and counted seven of the eight spread out on the street, talking to residents. They turned and pointed to the store where he'd purchased water and food.

Parked at the side of a street a few blocks north stood a weathered farm truck half full of green bananas, the driver squatting on the ground, drawing figures

83

in the dust, talking to another man.

One of the armed men shouted to them.

The men straightened and waved toward the truck.

The gunman nosed around it, peered inside the cab and into the back where the fruit was piled high. When he'd satisfied himself there was nothing of interest in the truck, he moved on and the men squatted again to their drawings in the dust.

Irish had an idea and hurried back to where he'd left Claire.

She rose from her position in the shadow of the ruins and hurried to meet him. "Are they still there?"

"Yes, and from what I saw, they're asking about us. It won't be long before they're directed to this location. We have to leave the Land Rover. Driving it out of town with the men on the main road would be too dangerous. But I have another idea."

"I'm all ears."

"Follow me." He led her through the alleys and less-traveled streets, backs against the walls, moving from building to building. When he neared the road where the banana truck was parked, he paused. The driver stood, nodding to the man he'd been talking with and headed for the driver's door.

"It's now or never." He grabbed Claire's hand.

"We're riding in a banana truck?"

Irish took off running, pulling her along with him. The truck's engine grumbled and coughed, spewing a thick black fog of diesel fumes, perfect to provide a modicum of concealment as he lifted Claire, bag and all, and set her in the truck.

He leaped up beside her and pulled her close to the stacks of bananas, dragging down several heavy stems to place behind them.

"Lie flat," he whispered.

Claire dropped to the bed of the truck and made herself as small as possible behind a growing stack of banana stems bunched with bananas.

The truck engine settled into a loud roar and jerked forward. Irish dropped down beside her, flattening himself behind the bananas as the vehicle pulled out onto the main street.

Through a gap in the bunches of bananas, Irish spotted a few of the armed men rushing in the direction he'd driven the Land Rover. Four remained in the street, shouting at the residents, brandishing their guns.

Leaving the Land Rover had been a

risk. He didn't like being without dedicated transportation, but he hadn't had much choice.

"Think they will catch up and search this truck?" Claire whispered.

"Maybe. But one of the men already searched it. With only an hour to the border, I'll bet this truck is going to Djibouti."

"Could we cross the border in the truck?"

He heard the tension in her voice and kept his calm. "They'll be checking the cargo. We'll drop out of it when we get close."

For the next hour, they bumped along in the back of the banana truck as the road led closer to their destination.

Irish prayed the crossing would be uneventful, he'd rejoin his team and they'd put this disaster behind them.

Unfortunately, reaching their destination would be the end of the adventure with the beautiful doctor. Irish would be on his way back to home base in Little Creek, Virginia. Claire sat up in the back of the truck, breathing diesel fumes and choking on the dust the truck spun up behind it, her thoughts churning through all that had happened. From helping villagers, to treating the al-Shabaab, almost being raped and now on the run with an all-too-sexy SEAL through potentially hostile territory, she had to admit her life had changed dramatically.

What worried her was the image of all the dead in the remote village and the whereabouts of her colleague, Dr. Jamo. As soon as she got to someplace where she could get help, the better. Whatever had decimated the village could spread to others. The sooner she notified the powers that be, whether the CDC, WHO or some other organization, she had to raise awareness to prevent what could turn into a pandemic and wipe out the entire continent of Africa if left unchecked.

She must have fallen asleep. When the truck rumbled to a stop, she felt lips brush hers in a soft caress.

"We're here," Irish whispered against her ear.

Claire sat up and rubbed the sleep from her eyes.

They were in an urban area, surrounded by people in vehicles and on foot. The hour was near dusk. Everyone looked tired and dusty, similar to the way Claire felt. What she wouldn't give for a cool shower and shampoo.

Irish climbed down from the truck and held out his arms. "We'd better continue on foot."

"I have my passport, but what about you?" she asked.

"I'll see you to the border guards and leave you there."

"How will you get across?" The thought of splitting up didn't sit well with Claire. Irish had been her rock, her protector. Without him, she was a lone woman in a strange country. And not knowing where he'd be, or whether he'd be caught, made her nervous.

"If we had time, I'd stay and try to push the issue. As it is, I'll make sure you get through. Then I'll find you on the other side." He pulled her into his arms and kissed her soundly. "Don't worry about me. Once you're in Djibouti, if I'm not there right away, don't wait. Catch a ride to the Djibouti International Airport. Camp Lemonnier is located there. Ask for the Joint Special Operations Command. I'll meet you there."

The more he talked of leaving her, the tighter the knot grew in her belly. She'd never felt safer than with Irish. Even when they'd been chased by the al-Shabaab. He was the highly trained fighter. Not her.

"Okay?" He raised her hand to his lips and stared into her eyes.

Claire's heart fluttered against her

ribs. Despite her misgivings about going through the border crossing alone, she nodded. "I'm okay. But promise me...I'll see you on the other side." Her fingers tightened in his.

"Count on it." He grinned. "I'll be watching you. If anything happens, I'll be there for you." Then he kissed her lips and disappeared into the crowd.

Knowing Irish would be watching her passage through the border crossing gave Claire a little more confidence. She pulled her passport out of the satchel and waited while four ramshackle trucks pulled forward, one of them being the banana truck she and Irish had stowed away on.

After the banana truck pulled through the crossing, it was her turn. She handed her passport to the guard with the military rifle and waited.

The guard stared at her passport and said something in Arabic.

Claire understood enough to realize he was asking for her papers. Pretending she didn't understand, she pointed to her bag and said the Arabic word for doctor.

With a frown, the guard called out to the man standing at the doorway to the guard shack.

He came over and took the satchel from Claire and rummaged through it, pulling out her stethoscope, laughing as he fit them in his ears.

Claire held her tongue and fought to keep from snatching back her things from the guard. She wanted to turn and find Irish's face in the crowd of people. Just when her nerves reached a breaking point, she saw the guards look past her to the road she'd arrived on.

Turning enough to glance behind her, Claire sucked in a breath, her heart leaping to her throat.

A truckload of Somali rebels rolled into the crowd. People scattered to get away, crying out.

The guards shoved the bag and Claire's passport at her and waved her through, raising their rifles to the ready position in the face of the oncoming truck.

With her clearance to pass through, Claire gathered her head scarf tighter around her face and hurried past the guards toward the banana truck, praying she could catch up to him before he left. From the way the other vehicles were taking off, the drivers wanted away from there before the rebels started causing trouble.

Claire walked fast, without turning back. She had almost reached the passenger door to the banana truck when she heard a shout behind her. Grabbing the handle on the side of the truck, she stepped up on the running board and called out in Arabic, "Please, take me to Djibouti International Airport." She shot a quick glance toward the border, praying Irish had found another way through farther along. Like he'd said, she couldn't stand around and wait. Not with rebel forces converging on the border patrol.

The driver waved at her, shaking his head.

Refusing to take no for an answer, Claire yanked open the door, shoved aside the trash on the passenger seat and slid inside, slamming the door behind her.

Another shout rose from the guards.

Claire glanced in the side mirror.

The rebels yelled at the guards, brandishing their weapons. The guards shook their heads and pointed toward the trucks leaving.

Her heart lodged in her throat, Claire ducked lower, praying the rebels and the guards hadn't seen which truck she'd climbed into. The driver beside her yelled, his Arabic too fast and garbled for her to translate. She didn't need a translation to know he wasn't happy she'd gotten in his truck, especially with the rebels behind them starting their way.

In Arabic, she said, "Go."

The driver shoved his shift in gear, popped the clutch and the engine died.

Holy crap. Claire could drive a manual transmission better. At this rate, the rebels would be pulling them out of the truck before they'd gone two feet.

A loud explosion ripped the air, shaking the ground beneath the truck.

Claire ducked, fully expecting the rebels had fired something horrible in their direction. In the side mirror, she watched as the rebels who'd been on their way toward the trucks most recent across the border, had dropped to their haunches, turning, their rifles aiming back across the border into Somalia.

A billowing, black column of smoke rose into the desert air from a burning vehicle.

The rebels turned and ran back across the border to where the fire burned in their truck. They shouted to each other and fired their weapons into the air.

With the knot in her chest easing, Claire smiled. That move had Irish written all over it. He'd created a diversion so that she could get safely away.

Starting the engine, the banana truck driver shifted into gear and eased his foot off the clutch. The truck surged forward, jerkily, and headed north on the coastal highway to Djibouti City.

Claire glanced in the mirror, praying Irish found a ride and that she'd see him very soon.

Chapter Six

AFTER HE LEFT Claire in the line, Irish had ducked behind a building. From his vantage point, he could see the border crossing and the road leading up to it from the south. He'd noticed the truckload of rebels as soon as they rolled into the small border town. Their faces were hidden behind red plaid or green scarves.

Meanwhile, the guards at the border crossing played with the items in Claire's doctor bag.

Thankfully, it was a busy day at the border. The truckload of rebels was forced to slow their approach.

When they all jumped from the truck and advance on the border guards, Claire was waved through.

She didn't wait around, moving through as soon as she got clearance.

"Smart lass," Irish whispered beneath his breath. But she wouldn't be safe for long. Just because she'd crossed the border into another country didn't mean squat to the rebels. They didn't respect borders, going after whatever they wanted. If they were after Claire, they wouldn't stop until they captured her.

Irish ducked into a shop, paid a man for his headscarf, wrapped it around his head and neck and hurried outside again. Slipping a package of matches from his pocket. With all the attention at the border where the guards argued with the rebels, no one saw the man stuffing a wad of fabric into the gas tank of the rebels' truck. If anyone did, they weren't saying anything as Irish lit a match, catching the tail of the fabric wad on fire. When he was certain it would stay lit, he backed away, slipping into the crowd, detaching himself when he reached a building and hurried around it, between two more and emerged on the other side of the loosely guarded border. He was angling toward the trucks heading north when the explosion shook the ground beneath him.

On the road, he spied the banana truck he and Claire had hitched a ride on and almost smiled. If he wasn't mistaken, the woman with the bright turquoise shash glancing out the passenger window was none other than Claire Boyette, amazing doctor and adventurer.

With all the attention on the burning vehicle on the Somali side of the border, no one made a sound when the man dressed in black leaped aboard the back of a banana truck and settled in for the long ride on a dusty road north to Djibouti City.

He leaned back against the stems of bananas and watched the black smoke from the vehicle fire climb into the sky and dissipate. He'd gotten lucky. If a crowd hadn't been at the border that day, he and Claire might not have made it across.

As long as the rebels didn't commandeer another vehicle, the banana truck and its occupants would make it safely to the city in less than forty minutes.

Those forty minutes in the back of the banana truck dragged by. The sun traveling toward the western horizon was still hot enough to make him sweat, even with the air stirred up by the vehicle's movement. Irish had plenty of time to think about what had happened. He prayed he'd find his team safe at the Joint Special Operations Command headquarters. Hopefully, the men of the downed helicopter had found their way back. He couldn't wait to find out how they'd escaped the al-Shabaab rebels.

When the truck finally pulled to a stop, Irish was happy to find himself at the entrance gate to Camp Lemonnier. He jumped from the back of the truck and hurried to the passenger door.

Claire offering her thanks to the driver and turned to get down when she spied him. Her eyes rounded and her face lit. "How did you get here?"

He held out his hands, caught her around the waist and pulled her against him. "The same way you did." He let her body slide down his until her feet touched the ground.

"I didn't think you'd make it out of there so soon."

"I told you I'd catch up to you."

She glanced around the side of the truck as the driver shifted into drive and pulled away. "But how…"

"I hung with a bunch of bananas."

Her smile widened and she chuckled. "And I worried about you for the past forty minutes."

Irish poked a thumb toward his chest. "Who me? I'm a SEAL. We have ways of making things happen."

"Especially when it involves blowing stuff up?" She winked and then glanced toward the buildings. "Do you think they'll let me on base?"

"They have to. You're with me." He took her hand in his and strode toward the gate guards.

Irish didn't even bother trying to argue his way onto the compound. He told the guard to call the commander of

97

Joint Special Operations and tell them "Irish is waiting to be rescued at the gate."

The army military policeman stood with his rifle at the ready while his buddy entered the hut and placed the call. Five minutes later, a HUMMV arrived and four SEALs piled out. Tuck, Big Bird and Fish rushed through the gate and enveloped him in a bone-crushing group hug.

His eyes stinging, Irish hugged them back.

"Man, we thought you were a dead man," Gator said, limping toward him, leaning on a single crutch.

The guys backed away and let Gator in to pound Irish on the back.

"Me? You were the one that ate a bullet."

Gator limped back a step. "Just a flesh wound. I'll be runnin' circles around you by morning."

"Yeah, right. Did they replace your leg with a bionic one because you can't run circles around me without a bullet in your leg."

"Are we standing out in the hot sun, or are you coming in for a beer and a shower?" Tuck waved his hand in front of his nose. "You smell."

"Yeah, we want to hear how you found your way back home." Big Bird wrapped an arm around his shoulder and aimed him for the guard shack.

The grin left Irish's face, and he stepped out of Big Bird's arm. "About that. Nice of you to leave me there."

"Dude, we were lucky to get off the ground loaded to the gills in one helicopter. We staged a raid for the next night. Lo and behold, Umar's camp had disbanded, picked up and left maybe minutes before we got there."

Irish snorted. "Yeah, we stirred up a hornet's nest getting away. Which reminds me, I'd like you to meet the person responsible for my rescue, no thanks to you guys." He reached out, snagged Claire's arm and pulled her close to him.

His buddies all turned toward her, brows rising as she pushed the scarf off her head.

She held out her hand to Gator. "I'm Dr. Claire Boyette."

"I should have waited to have my leg looked at," Gator said with a wink.

Fish elbowed him. "You better not let Mitchell hear you talking like that." He offered his hand to Claire. "Thanks for rescuing Irish's ass. Don't know what we'd do without his fake accent to keep it colorful around here."

Her brows arched. "He tells me it's real."

Fish snorted. "Yeah, right."

"Trust Irish to find the pretty lady." Tuck took her hand next. "Pleasure to meet you."

Big Bird's cheeks reddened as he took Claire's hand and muttered, "Nice to meet you."

By the time all four of his welcoming committee shook Claire's hand, Irish was ready to jump in the middle and tell them to knock it off. She was *his* girl. Only she wasn't. Claire didn't belong to anyone and he'd better remember that. Just because they'd made love like a couple of teenagers in the back of the Land Rover didn't mean she belonged to him.

"Did I hear the mention of a shower?" Claire asked, hooking her hand through Irish's arm.

His chest swelled. She might not be his, but by taking his arm like she had, it sure felt like she was. "Come on, we're bound to find both food and water."

Tuck slid into the driver's seat, Gator rode shotgun, leaving the three men to sprawl across the backseat. Claire chewed on her bottom lip. "I can wait for the next vehicle."

"No way." Irish patted his lap. "Come on. I don't bite…much."

She gave him a sexy glance from beneath her lashes and slid onto his lap.

Dusty and in need of a shower, Claire

100

was still the sexiest female Irish had the pleasure of knowing. He wondered if they'd get time alone again, or if this would be the last close contact he'd have. With her sitting on his lap, her bottom rubbing against his crotch, the inevitable was bound to happen and his groin tightened. *Damn.* If the guys noticed his pants were tented and he was sporting a boner, he'd never hear the end of it.

Claire wrapped her arm around his neck and held on as the HUMMV lurched forward, stirring up dust behind them. The short drive to the headquarters building was over too soon.

Sliding across him one more time, Claire exited the vehicle and waited.

Irish stood, adjusted his trousers and prayed the debriefing wouldn't last long. He wanted to get Claire alone.

Dusk was settling in as Tuck ushered Irish and Claire through the door to the command center.

An hour later, after telling all she knew about the al-Shabaab takeover of Samada and her work on Umar, Claire told them how Dr. Jamo had been loaded into a vehicle and driven away.

She turned to Irish when she said, "And we need to notify the CDC and the World Health Organization about the village."

Irish told them of the entire village full of dead people and its approximate location.

The commander, U.S. Army Colonel Mathis, shot a glance at his assistant. "Get the guys at Langley on it. Have them pull up the satellite images. They'll notify the powers that be and have them investigate."

"What about Dr. Jamo? Can you have Langley do something about getting him out of al-Shabaab's hands?"

Colonel Mathis's lips pressed together. "I'll have Intel do some digging. If we can locate him, we'll do our best to extract him."

Claire gave a wan smile. "Thank you."

"If that's all you have, Dr. Boyette, Petty Officer Sjodin will escort you to billeting where you will be assigned quarters.

Eyebrows raised, Claire glanced toward Irish.

He nodded. "I'll find you."

Big Bird escorted her out of the building.

The commander waited until the door closed behind Claire and Big Bird before he started pacing. "So, our strike to take out Umar failed since the good doctor was forced to patch him up."

Irish shook his head. "At gun point."

"What are the chances of finding Dr. Jamo?"

"I have no idea." Irish knew finding her friend meant a lot to Claire. "The doctors were helping the native people. If it's at all in our capabilities to find and extract him, I'd volunteer to go. Claire— Dr. Boyette—is no different than members of this team. She won't give up on her colleague any more than we'd give up on one of our own."

"We'll do the best we can." Colonel Mathis gave him a steady stare. "I'm glad you made it back alive."

Irish left the command center and hurried toward the stacked containerized housing units, the huge, metal shipping containers that had been converted into air-conditioned living quarters. The team had been assigned rooms on the front end of the operation where Irish had left his gear what felt like a lifetime ago. In fact, only a few days had passed. So much had happened in that short time.

He'd met an amazing woman. Who would have thought he'd find someone in the heart of Africa who could capture his attention as much as Claire had?

All he knew was that he couldn't wait to see her again. His first stop was the housing container Big Bird had been assigned.

"Miss me already?" Big Bird asked from his position sprawled on a cot in the cool air.

"Where is she?" Irish asked.

Big Bird grinned and rattled off the number of the unit and the row he could find it in. "But she's probably in the mess hall." He wrinkled his nose. "Dude, you really should shower before you show up at her door."

Taking Big Bird's advice, Irish grabbed clean pants, a T-shirt and a towel and headed for the shower facility. Ten minutes later, scrubbed free of three days of dust and grime, he finger-combed his damp hair and glanced at his face in the metal mirror, deciding it was worth the effort to scrape the three-day-old beard off his chin, nicking himself in his hurry to be done.

By the time he entered the chow hall, it was past normal dinner hours and the place was fairly empty.

Tuck and Dustman sat at a table on the far end, their backs to Irish. Not until he got closer did he see they were talking with Claire, and she was smiling at something they said.

A stab of something raw and angry hit him square in the gut. Could he be jealous of his teammates? Both were in committed relationships with women back in the States. They shouldn't be interested in Claire. But when her blue-gray eyes sparkled with laughter and her smile lit her face like sunshine on a cloudy day, how could anyone not fall in love with her?

Love?

Irish shook himself. He'd prided himself on playing the field, asserting he had no right to be exclusive with one woman when he could make so many more happy. Then why did all others fade from memory when he stared at Claire across the room?

She glanced up, her gaze meeting his, and her smile widened.

Irish's heart skipped several beats and then raced on. He crossed the room without noting anything in his path, nearly tripping over a chair.

Fuck. He had to get a grip. A woman should not have the power to derail him so completely.

"Aren't you getting something to eat?" Claire asked as he neared the table. She looked down at her empty tray. "I'm afraid I couldn't wait."

"We told her you could be all night if the C.O. got long-winded," Tuck said.

"You don't have to wait on me."

"No, I wanted to." Claire's face softened. "These gentlemen were just keeping me company until you arrived."

"And, now that you're here, I'm sure we have something important to do." Tuck rose and backhanded Dustman in the chest. "Don't we?"

Dustman frowned. "We do?"

Tuck shook his head. "Give Irish time alone with the good doctor. I'm sure they have a lot to catch up on in the time they've been apart."

"She saw him an hour ago," Dustman argued, a frown marring his expression.

Tuck grabbed Dustman by the back of shirt and forced him to his feet. "Don't you have someone to talk to back home?"

Dustman grinned. "I sure do. I told Jenna I'd call at..." He glanced down at his watch, "Crap! Right now." He leaped out of his seat. "Nice talking to you. I'll have the medic check on that hangnail before it gets worse. Thanks for the advice." Dustman left, Tuck following close behind.

"Get some food," Claire said. "I'm not going anywhere."

His stomach grumbled, reminding him they hadn't had much to eat in the past couple of days. "I'll be right back."

Thankfully, the chow hall remained open twenty-four hours. With personnel operating in shifts, people were headed to work as others got off and lunch could be at sixteen hundred, midnight, two in the morning or noon—whatever time the individual had to eat chow.

Loading his tray with two grilled chicken breasts, salad and vegetables, he figured he was eating pretty healthy until he passed the dessert section and couldn't walk past the chocolate cake with rich fudge icing. Two glasses of ice water and a cup of coffee balanced on his tray, and he was on his way back to Claire.

She smiled when she saw what he'd put on his tray. "I think I had the same— only one chicken breast. The chocolate cake was to die for."

Nodding, he shoveled several bites of food into his mouth and chewed. He wanted to know about Claire, things they didn't have time to discuss on the road. Where was home when she wasn't in Africa? Did she have family back in the states? What was her favorite color? Did she like dogs? Some of those things appeared unimportant but seemed to define a person.

What he knew of Claire already impressed him—her dedication to the craft of healing, her bravery in the face of incredible danger, the fact she fought back when a man tried to rape her instead of breaking down and crying. She was smart, caring, passionate and had an amazing body. He couldn't look up into her eyes at that moment, or she'd see how much he craved being with her again. Instead, he scooped up another forkful of food and enjoyed the act of chewing.

"Now that we're back in relative civilization, what are you doing from here?"

Claire glanced down at the food on his fork. "I'm going to find Dr. Jamo."

Irish's hand froze halfway to his mouth. "You're doing what?"

"Find Dr. Jamo." She looked up, capturing his gaze with her clear steady blue-gray stare.

Setting down his fork, his appetite squelched, Irish leaned forward. "Assuming you had the transportation and the firepower behind you, how will you find him?"

"I'll go back to Samada and start asking questions there."

"If Umar discovers you, he'll kill you." Irish shook his head. "Worse. He'll do heinous things to you as a lesson to others, and then kill you."

A shiver shook her body and she glanced away. Apparently, the attempted rape in the hut in Samada had made more of an impact on her than he'd thought. Still, Claire squared her shoulders and lifted her chin. "I'm going. The longer we wait to rescue him, the less chance we have of finding him alive."

"Umar would be stupid to kill him. There are few enough doctors in Somalia to waste one with a bullet."

"Then why would they kill me?" she asked, her voice firm, though she appeared less than confident.

"You got away, and a couple of his men died in the process."

"I didn't kill them."

"You escaped with one of the men who ruined his day and filled him with shrapnel."

"I pulled out the shrapnel," she pointed out, though her voice trailed at the end. She reached for Irish's hands. "Don't you see? I can't leave Dr. Jamo to those murderers."

Irish nodded. "I wouldn't leave my team members to them. But wandering back into Samada won't do much good. You heard my team. They went back. Umar bugged out."

"Someone had to have seen where they went."

"You can't do it alone. Let the guys at Langley do their magic and find Umar using their fancy satellites. That way will be faster and not nearly as dangerous."

Claire scrubbed a hand over her face. "I hate the thought of them torturing Dr. Jamo. He's a good man, concerned about the well-being of his people."

"I'm concerned about him, too, but going off half-cocked won't help him." He held her hands in his. "Give the brains time to look."

She sighed. "I don't feel right being clean, fed and sleeping in comfort when he's out there suffering."

"You have a big heart, Dr. Boyette." He smiled and lifted his fork. His appetite might have waned, but he needed nourishment to sustain his body through whatever action might present itself. When he'd finished the cake, he stacked their two trays and carried them to the drop point.

He held out his hand to Claire. They left the chow hall and walked out into the balmy dessert night, the moon shining overhead and casting them in dark blue light. "Come on, I'll walk you to your room."

"You mean my box?" She laughed. "I must say, the space is a lot nicer on the inside than it appears on the outside."

"And it beats sleeping in the dirt, or on hard metal in the back of an SUV."

Her hand tightened in his. "I don't know. The back of the SUV had its advantages."

"It did, didn't it?" Irish pulled her arm through his, bringing her body close enough he inhaled the scent of her shampoo. "You smell good."

Her light laugh warmed his heart. "Nice pick-up line."

Irish puffed out his chest. "I know exactly what to say to sweep the lasses off their feet."

"Uh huh." Though her voice dripped sarcasm, she leaned into him, resting her cheek against his arm.

God, he loved the way her body melded to his and the way she kicked at the gravel, in no hurry to leave his side.

All too soon, they arrived at the row of boxes stacked three high and stopped in front of the ground-level container she'd been assigned.

Not wanting to push her when she'd already been through so much, Irish brushed her hair off her cheek and kissed her. His tongue swept past her teeth to slide the length of hers, hungrily tasting, twisting and turning. When he broke it off, he stepped back, breathing a bit erratically, his body on fire with desire.

"Would you like to come in?"

"No. Really, you need sleep after what we went through today."

She smiled and leaned against the doorframe. "Remember that rain check you promised?"

Irish's heart leaped at her words and

the way she looked at him with challenge in the tilt of her chin. Never mind the strict rules of no fraternizing on the military installation during deployment. He was a man willing to take risks. "Darlin', I'm all about keeping my promises."

She turned with a sway of her hips and a sexy smile.

He held the door, wondering how he'd gotten so lucky as to fall out of a helicopter. Rather than look that gift horse in the mouth, he followed her inside.

Chapter Seven

CLAIRE HAD NEVER seduced a man in her life. With Irish, the behavior came natural. Every red blood cell in her body sizzled with anticipation, desire curling at her core, sending tingles outward like a chemical reaction.

Eager to get the party started, she pulled the borrowed T-shirt over her head and tossed it over the end of the singlewide cot. Braless, she turned to face him and dropped the oversized scrubs bottoms Big Bird had appropriated from medical supply. She stood before him completely naked. Her only undergarments draped over a makeshift clothesline at the end of the room, after the thorough washing she'd given them while she showered.

Irish took her hands in his and held them wide, his gaze sweeping over her body, his eyes flaring as his gaze skimmed over her breasts and lower to that tuft of hair at the juncture of her thighs. "You're a very lovely lass."

"And you are far too overdressed." She tugged her hands to free them from his grip. The longer he stared the more

113

self-conscious she became.

"I can remedy that." Releasing her hands, he stripped, flinging his clothes to the corners of the room until he stood before her as naked as she was.

Claire's heart thundered and her core clenched. This time when they made love, she'd take her time, learn every inch of his body, memorizing it for when they were no longer together.

Thoughts of the future threatened to tinge her rising passion with a pall of sadness.

Irish touched a finger beneath her chin and lifted her face. "One minute you're all fire and passion. The next, you look like a puppy someone kicked. What are you thinking about?"

"I want tonight to be special."

"Why just tonight?"

She slid her hands across the hard plains of his chest, reveling in the strength beneath her fingertips, tweaking one small brown nipple. "After tonight, you might be headed back to the States."

"Or not."

She gave him a weak smile and pressed her lips where her fingers had been, tonguing the tight bud. "The point is, you have your life back in the States and wherever the Navy sends you. I have my life here in Africa." And she'd stay as long as needed to find and free Dr. Jamo. What happened after that was a mystery.

"Have you ever considered moving back Stateside?" He cupped her cheeks in his palms and lifted her face to his.

"I don't have anyone back there."

"No friends or relatives?"

"No one." *Doesn't that sound pathetic?*

He pressed his lips to hers in a soft, gentle kiss. "You have me."

Her pulse sped, her heart tripping over every beat. "We just met. You don't even know me."

"I know you're smart, brave and beautiful." He kissed her again, his tongue pushing through her teeth to toy with hers.

She curled her fingers into the hair at the back of his neck and drew him closer.

When Irish raised his head, he stared down into her eyes. "Claire, I don't want this to be the last time we see each other."

She laughed, the sound closer to a sob than anything else. "We might as well live on different planets. A relationship would be completely out of the question." Even if she wanted it. And she wanted it, more than she ever realized. Working in Africa, she'd made friends among her colleagues and the people she'd helped, but something had always been missing. She didn't have anyone she could share her joys and sorrows with. She didn't have anyone with whom she could build hopes and dreams. Her parents had been the center of her life for so long. When they'd died, she'd thought she'd lost everything. Her grandmother's death the following year left her with no one to call her own.

Being with Irish reminded her of all she'd been missing. Their careers put them at a distinct disadvantage.

"Perhaps the past few days together have been nothing more than a challenge we had to overcome. Whatever feelings we have for each other are a manifestation of sharing difficult times together." Being rational would save her emotions. "If we were in a position we could date, we might find each other boring or annoying."

Irish pressed a finger to her lips, quelling her rush of words. "You're overthinking this." He skimmed his hands over her shoulders and down her arms, coming to rest at her hips. Digging his fingers into her ass, he pressed her against his hardening cock. "For tonight, let's live in the moment. We can talk all we want tomorrow. But know this, I don't plan on tonight being the end. It's only the beginning of what could be between us."

"You're right," she said, wrapping her arms around him, pulling him closer where her breasts rubbed against his chest.

His brows dipped. "About which part?"

She smiled. "I'm overthinking this. We have tonight. Let's not waste it." Pushing thoughts of a future without Irish to the back of her mind, Claire melted against him, loving the feel of his naked skin against hers. Sliding her leg up the back of his, she pressed her sex against his thick muscle, his coarse hairs making her crazy, wanting more.

Irish scooped her up by the backs of her thighs.

She wrapped her legs around his waist and eased down over him, taking his length into her channel.

He closed his eyes, his arms cinching around her, his cock thrusting up into her. "You. Are. Amazing..." Backing her against the metal door, he thrust into her again.

Another first for her. She'd never made love against a door, or a wall, for that matter. The cool metal on her back made a stark contrast to the fire radiating between their heated bodies. She rested her hands on his shoulders and rode him, pushing up and sliding down with each of his thrusts until her pussy clenched and a tidal wave of sensations engulfed her, sweeping her away.

One last thrust, and Irish held her hard against him, his staff buried to the hilt, long thick and throbbing.

Her mind mush, her legs shaking, Claire laughed shakily. "That was incredible."

"Darlin', you inspire me." He winked and carried her to the single bed, laying her down first, and then slipping in beside her. Irish was a big man, his muscles taking up much of the thin mattress.

Claire didn't mind. It meant they were forced to lay close together, bodies touching. She slid her hand across his chest and up behind his neck. "Kiss me," she demanded. If this was the last time they'd be together, she wanted to pack away as many memories as she could.

In the early hours of the morning, Irish rose from the bed.

Claire blinked open her eyes. "Is it morning?"

"Not yet," he whispered. He'd wanted to slip from her quarters without disturbing her, mostly out of self-preservation. If she woke, he would be hard-pressed to resist holding her again.

Arms over her head, Claire stretched.

Her naked body tempted the saint right out of Irish. He sat on the side of the little bed and smoothed a hand over her shoulder and down to cup her breast.

She covered his hand with hers and squeezed. "Stay."

He tweaked her nipple between his thumb and forefinger. "It's against the installation regulations to fraternize here. I need to leave before someone sees me."

"Are you sure you can't stay for one more round?" Her hand guided his to the patch of hair covering her mons. She pressed his fingers between her folds and sucked in a deep, shuddering breath. "Please."

Who was he kidding? He was no match for Claire the Temptress, her body warm from sleep, her sex wet and inviting. Thrusting his finger into her, he swirled and then dragged it up to stroke that sliver of flesh that made her so very crazy.

She dug her heels into the mattress and raised her hips, urging him to continue.

He did, stroking, flicking and strumming her until she cried out, her body quivering with her release.

Irish rolled on top of her and thrust deep inside, his cock encased in her warmth and wetness. He could die now and have known perfection and complete satisfaction. Rising up on his hands, he pumped in and out, increasing the rhythm until the little cot shook, the springs squealing. One last thrust and he buried himself.

Claire wrapped her legs around him, digging her heels into his buttocks.

God, she felt so damned good, Irish hated when he had to finally withdraw.

Slowly lowering her legs, Claire smiled up at him. "That wasn't so bad, now, was it?"

"You had me at please." He bent to capture her lips in a soul-defining kiss. "It'll be daylight soon."

She stretched, her stomach rumbling. "Do you have time to eat an early breakfast?"

"Until my commander assigns me a new mission or redeploys us Stateside, I'm free."

"I'll join you for breakfast in ten minutes." She sat up, pushing back her hair from her face, the action making her breasts jut out.

"Keep that up, and we won't leave this room all day."

"Keep what up?" She blinked quickly.

He reached out and tweaked her nipple. "Move. Breathe. Flaunt your gorgeous, naked body. Hell, all you have to do is stand there. A man can only take so much."

She grinned. "I'd say, let's go for

another round," she eyed his still hard cock, "but I'm hungry for food." Claire rose from the bed and gathered her clothing. "Maybe after?"

"You're on." He slapped her bare ass, shoved his feet into his trousers and slipped on his tennis shoes. As he pulled his shirt over his head, he said, "See you in ten minutes."

He left her in her room and stepped out into the near-darkness of predawn. It wouldn't be long before the sun rose and scorched the land and the people who dared to live and work on it. Irish didn't care how hot it was, he only knew he was having breakfast with Claire. He'd take one minute, one hour, and one day at a time. He refused to look too far into the future and the moment he'd have to say goodbye.

Claire found the latrine and performed her morning ablutions. Without a curling iron or blow dryer, there wasn't much she could do to improve her hair, besides pulling it back and arranging it into a French braid. Wearing a T-shirt and scrub pants and no make-up, she wasn't exactly looking her best, but her appearance was the best she could manage. Actually, she'd never felt more beautiful than when she'd stood

121

naked in front of Irish. The hungry gleam in his eyes fed her desire and made her feel like the most lovely and desirable woman in the world. And lucky. Irish was a helluva gorgeous specimen of man. From his broad shoulders and iron abs to his narrow waist and sexy ass. Yeah, she was lucky to have had the opportunity to make love with a man who could be every girl's wet dream.

Hurrying back to her containerized housing unit, Claire dropped off the trial-sized tube of toothpaste and her toothbrush before she hurried for the mess hall. Around her, the sun peeked over the eastern horizon, and the camp came alive. Men and women dressed in shorts and T-shirts spilled out of their containerized living quarters, stretching before a morning run. Others wore uniforms and headed to their duty stations.

As Claire crossed the main road leading into and out of the garrison, she did a double take.

A white truck was parked beside one of the administration buildings, and it had a familiar logo on the side door.

Claire's footsteps faltered and came to a complete halt when the image of a green flying dove came into focus.

At first, she thought it was the same

vehicle that had taken Dr. Jamo, but then she recalled an SUV had driven away with her colleague. This vehicle wasn't a Land Rover. Nobody was in the truck and it was parked outside what appeared to be a medical clinic.

Her heart pounding, Claire walked through the clinic door. In the back of her mind, she harbored the hope of finding Dr. Jamo inside, smiling and laughing with the staff, explaining some of the natural remedies they used in Somalia when medications weren't available.

Only Dr. Jamo's dark face and graying hair wasn't what she found. Instead, she saw a coal-black man in a green uniform waiting at the desk.

A young woman in a U.S. Army desert camouflage uniform stood behind the counter. "It'll be at least thirty minutes before we have the results for you. If you'd like to take a seat, I'll call you when it's ready."

The man nodded and took a seat in the waiting room.

"May I help you, ma'am?" The woman behind the counter asked Claire.

"No, I think I'm in the wrong building," Claire said, her voice barely above a whisper. Who was that black man, and what connection did he have to do with the people who'd taken Dr. Jamo?

"What building were you looking for?"

"The mess hall?" Claire said, knowing perfectly well where it was.

"You're not far. It's a couple buildings over." The female soldier gave her the directions with another smile.

Claire left the building. She half-walked, half-ran to the mess hall, bursting through the door, her gaze searching for Irish.

"Hey," a voice said beside her.

She turned and fell into Irish's arms.

He held her for a minute then pushed her to arms' length. "Are you all right? You look like you've seen a ghost."

"There's a white truck outside that looks similar to the one that took Dr. Jamo." She grabbed his hand and dragged him toward the exit.

Irish followed her to the corner of the medical clinic where the truck still stood.

"There." She pointed, breathing hard, her heart pumping blood through her so fast she was dizzy. "It isn't an SUV, but it's got the exact logo on the door panel."

"A flying dove." Irish studied the vehicle for a moment, then took her hand and led her toward the Special Operations Command center where they'd been debriefed the night before.

"I need to talk to Colonel Mathis," he said to the army sergeant at the front desk.

"I'll see if he's available."

"What's the problem?" Colonel Mathis emerged from the back office, followed by his assistant, an army captain.

"Dr. Boyette spotted a truck outside with a similar logo to the vehicle used to take away her colleague Dr. Jamo. Could we determine who owns the logo? Perhaps we can find out where they've taken Dr. Jamo."

The commander's brows furrowed. "Have you considered al-Shabaab might have stolen the truck?"

"Yes, sir." Irish squared his shoulders. "But if there's an even remote possibility they didn't steal it, and whoever owns the vehicle with the logos has something to do with Dr. Jamo's disappearance, I'd like to follow up on it."

"Fair enough." Colonel Mathis waved his assistant forward. "Captain Copeland, we need someone to make a subtle inquiry into the ownership of the logo."

"Yes, sir. I'll check into it," the captain said and hurried out of the building.

"Thank you, sir," Irish said. "We'll be in the chow hall, should you need to find us." He hustled Claire out of the command center and back toward the chow hall.

"I'm not hungry," Claire said, digging her heels into the dirt. "How can you eat at a time like this? If that company has anything to do with Dr. Jamo's kidnapping, I want to know immediately."

"We don't know someone from that company took him. And if we want to know more, we need to give the good captain a chance to inquire."

Claire shoved her hand through her hair. "What if he tips off the man and he leaves before we can find out where Dr. Jamo is?"

Irish touched her arm. "I seriously doubt the man in that clinic would know anything about Dr. Jamo."

"But if he doesn't, someone he works with might."

"I have an idea. Come with me to the mess hall, and I'll fill you in with the rest of the team."

Claire stopped resisting and followed Irish to the cafeteria, her gaze turning to the white truck up to the point they entered the chow hall, the building's walls cutting off her view. "What if that truck is going to the same place where they're holding Dr. Jamo? He'll be leaving in thirty minutes or less. Can't we follow it?" She faced him. "I know I sound crazy, but this might be our only lead."

"Darlin', we're surrounded by miles and miles of desert. You know that if we follow a vehicle across it, they are sure to see us. I have a better idea, but I need my buddy Swede's assistance." He found the majority of his team eating breakfast at a table in the far corner.

"Irish, Dr. Claire, join us," Tuck invited, scooting over to allow them to sit in the middle.

Claire liked the easy camaraderie among the team and the teasing way they treated each other. She had no doubt they would take a bullet for each other, but they didn't take each other too seriously when they had downtime.

"Swede," Irish started without preamble. "Did you bring along any of your gee-whiz gizmos?"

The tall man with pale blond hair seated directly across from Irish frowned. "What do you mean gee-whiz gizmos?"

"In particular, did you bring any GPS tracking devices?"

Swede sat back, smiling. "You know I come prepared for anything."

Irish lowered his voice and leaned across the table. "Including tracking a vehicle through the deserts and potentially the jungles of Africa?"

Swede's smile faded and his body tensed. "Why? Have we got a mission?"

The entire team leaned in to hear what Irish had to say.

"Not official. I'm not sure it has anything to do with anything, but if it does, we need to take this chance." He explained about Dr. Jamo and the white vehicles with the dove logo on the side door.

"Is that all you need?"

"For now. I might need you all to run interference for me should I need to bug out and find Dr. Jamo at a moment's notice."

"Count me in," Tuck said.

"Me, too," Big Bird agreed.

Everyone else piped in, offering his assistance.

"Thanks, but for now, I'd like to keep this goat rope to a minimum." Irish's jaw tightened. "If I go AWOL, I don't want any of you going down with me."

Claire bit her lip. She didn't like the idea of the guys getting in trouble.

"What's our timeframe?" Swede asked.

"Less than twenty minutes to plant the bug."

Swede leaped from his seat. "I'll be back."

"You gonna tell the C.O.?" Tuck asked.

Irish stared at his teammate. "Not if I

think it'll jeopardize the mission."

"Gotcha." Tuck glanced at the door to the mess hall. "There's Captain Copeland now."

Claire swiveled in her seat. Her head spun with everything happening so far, her hopes high that they'd be able to find Dr. Jamo and deliver him safely back to Djibouti.

Captain Copeland spotted her and headed toward the group at the table. "The company that truck belongs to is owned by the government of Ethiopia. It's an up-and-coming pharmaceutical company. They occasionally ask to use our medical lab facilities when they experience power issues."

"Power issues?" Tuck's brows wrinkled. "A pharmaceutical company with power issues?"

"A part of our ability to operate out of Djibouti means we have MOUs, memos of understanding, between local medical facilities," the captain explained.

"Ethiopia isn't local," Irish stated.

"That question's between Ethiopia and Djibouti." Captain Copeland straightened. "Colonel Mathis would like to speak with Chief Petty Officer O'Shea and Dr. Boyette as soon as possible." With that parting comment, the captain left the mess hall, probably expecting

Claire and Irish to follow.

When Irish didn't immediately rise, Claire remained seated, wondering what more he had to say to the others.

Irish faced Tuck. "You'll make sure the tracking device finds its way onto that vehicle?"

Tuck nodded. "Don't worry. Swede will take care of it. I'm going with you."

"Dr. Jamo helped save my life." Irish stood. "I'd like to return the favor."

Claire's heart swelled at Irish's words.

As they walked out of the mess hall, one of the SEALs stepped up beside her and held out his hand. "I'm Jack Fischer."

"The one they call Fish?" she asked as she clasped his hand.

He grinned. "That's me. Just wondered if you'd considered working as a doctor anywhere else but Africa?"

She glanced up into his face. "Why do you ask?"

Irish joined her. "His lady is a doctor, too."

Butterflies erupted in Claire's belly. Irish had intimated she was his lady. After their short time together, she hadn't expected any commitment from the man. But the loose connection felt good. "Where does she practice medicine?" Claire asked.

"She's founded a non-profit, floating

doctor boat."

"Boat?" *How does that work?*

"Yeah, they travel to Central and South America, providing services to people who can't afford or don't have access to good medical attention. They could always use another doctor on board."

"Thanks. I'll keep that in mind."

"She bases out of Norfolk when she's not touring south." Fish shrugged. "Just saying. They could use the help, should you decide Africa is too dangerous."

Irish snorted. "Not like Central and South America are terror free."

"No, they're not." Fish had the decency to blush. "But at least I get to see Natalie a few times during the year."

"Sounds interesting," Claire said, and meant it. To work alongside another female doctor doing what she loved most might be nice. Helping others who can't help themselves. But that was all assuming they rescued Dr. Jamo alive before the SEALs had to bug out on another mission somewhere else in the world.

What would it be like to come home to Virginia where the SEALs were based? She'd lived so long in Africa, the relocation would mean an adjustment to live in the States. The thought of having someone to come home to appealed to her more than she cared to admit.

If she took a job with the doctor boat, she might have a chance to get to know Irish when she was in port. She'd like that.

"Let's go see what the colonel wants." Irish rested his hand at the small of her back and guided her toward the Special Operations command center.

Tuck followed.

Claire prayed Colonel Mathis didn't put the kibosh on the potential rescue mission. She owed it to Dr. Jamo to get him out alive.

Chapter Eight

"I TAKE IT Captain Copeland gave you the information." Colonel Mathis stood in the briefing room, his hands on his hips, combat boots spread wide.

Irish nodded, unable to gauge the colonel's take on the information. "He did. The trucks belong to a pharmaceutical company out of Ethiopia."

The colonel watched as Tuck entered the room and closed the door behind him. "Good, I'm glad you came, Tuck." He stepped aside to reveal Gator seated at the table behind him. "Gator is up on the intel. I'll let him fill you in."

Tuck glanced toward Claire. "Does the good doctor need clearance to hear what you have to say?"

Claire tensed beside Irish.

The colonel glanced from Irish to Claire and back. "Since she was in Samada when the shit hit the fan, and she also pointed out the connection to the pharmaceutical company, we'll let the clearance slide this time." He tipped his head toward Gator.

"We got word from Langley that they think they found Umar. Satellite photos

133

indicate he might be at one of the Ethiopian pharmaceutical company's locations in the desert."

"You think he's working with them?" Claire asked. "Why?"

"Langley's been tracking a string of occurrences in a pattern on the border of Somalia and Ethiopia. It started with Umar's raids on outlying villages. Consensus was that at first, he shot all his victims, but a special team was sent in to the decimated villages after the attacks. They discovered the people didn't die by the usual bullet to the head or beheading. Their bodies and heads were intact. Every last one of them died of something else."

"Biological warfare?" Irish asked.

Claire gasped. "Like the village we passed through on our way here?"

Gator nodded. "They suspected the pharmaceutical company, but didn't have anything to go on until you identified the vehicle in Umar's camp as one similar to that of our weekly visitor to Camp Lemonnier."

Claire's face got even paler. "They could just as easily have brought whatever chemical or disease on the post."

Gator's lips thinned. "My first thought."

"The team that investigated the dead villagers sent photos of the blood

134

samples," Colonel Mathis said. "We have our medical lab technicians testing the blood of all those who came into contact with the courier. We've delayed him for the time being, claiming the tests he wanted run were taking longer than expected due to equipment malfunction."

A knock on the door interrupted their discussion.

"Enter," the colonel called out.

Captain Copeland opened the door and set one foot inside. "Negative on the blood samples. All clear."

"You can release the courier," Colonel Mathis said.

"We're feeding him now since his samples took so long. We'll have him out of here as soon as possible." Captain Copeland left the room, closing the door behind him.

"Which leads us to the next action," Mathis said.

Gator pushed to his feet, limped to a computer and clicked the mouse. A satellite photo popped up on a white screen behind the SEAL. "These are the images Langley sent." He clicked the mouse again and a map overlaid the satellite photo. Gator pointed to a spot on the map, in the middle of a desert. "This is the pharmaceutical company's factory. Note the field of white beside the structure. Those are solar panels they use to power the manufacturing processes."

Pointing to a different position in the rugged hills, Gator said, "And this is another building they've identified. Trucks from the factory move at night to this location. It is also the location to which they've tracked Umar."

Irish glanced from Gator to Colonel Mathis. "Why are you telling me all of this?"

Colonel Mathis tapped the screen over the building in the hills. "That also happens to be the location of Prince Yohannis's country palace, the favored son of the most powerful figure in Ethiopia and one of our allies in the region. He's a Harvard-educated chemical engineer with connections to some of the richest Saudi family members."

"In other words," Irish said, "we go in there, and we stir up an international incident."

"Exactly." Colonel Mathis paced the floor. "I'm usually a man who believes in playing by the rules. But if Yohannis is in cahoots with Umar, then we have a problem that will take more than diplomacy to resolve." He stared at the men in the room. "If you get my drift."

Irish's eyes narrowed. "I have a feeling a few Navy SEALs are going rogue tonight."

The colonel's lips curled into a wry twist. "Can't imagine that ever happens. Nor can I imagine the guard falling asleep on duty on the flight line where the 160th Night Stalkers keep a couple Black Hawks at the ready."

"And if we're caught, we're on our own," Gator finished.

Irish stared at the LT. "Sorry, old man, but you're grounded."

"It's just a nick," Gator protested.

"Can't have you slowing us down," Irish argued with a shake of his head.

"Now, I'm just stepping out of the room to ensure I don't hear a thing about any kind of defiant behavior among members of the Joint Special Operations Command." Mathis paused with his hand on the doorknob. "Keep the casualties to a minimum, but take out Umar once and for all."

Irish gave the commander a salute. "Yes, sir."

The colonel opened the door, and half of the team fell inside. The C.O. chuckled. "I think these might belong to you."

Big Bird, Dustman, Fish, Nacho and others poured through the door into the room and dropped into the chairs positioned around the conference table.

"Dr. Boyette, you might want to check in with the medical clinic and see how they are coming with the results on those samples," Tuck suggested.

Claire stood tall, her jaw set. "I want to stay and hear how we're getting into Yohannis's compound."

Tuck was already shaking his head. "Not *we*. You won't be going with the team, ma'am."

She frowned. "Why not? I know what Dr. Jamo looks like."

Irish nodded. "So do I. But this will be a military exercise. It'll be dangerous and you don't belong in the middle."

"What if someone is injured?" she argued. "I could act as the team medic."

"I'm sorry, Claire." Irish took her hands in his and pressed a kiss to her knuckles. "We travel light and fast. Having a female among us will distract us from our mission."

"I can help," she insisted.

"A lot of people here need your assistance. No use taking a bullet in hostile territory, depriving others of your healing touch."

Claire bit down on her bottom lip, her cheeks flushed, her eyes flashing.

Damn, she was sexy when she was angry. But under no circumstances would they take her with them. She would be a liability and make them lose focus on the mission. "Darlin', you can't go with us."

She nodded, her lips firming into a tight line. "I see."

Irish could tell she didn't see at all. If the stubborn tilt of her chin was any indication, she wasn't finished arguing, only waiting to get him alone to press her point.

"Dr. Boyette, you'll have to leave." Gator nodded toward the door. "We have work to do in order to get in to extract Dr. Jamo."

And neutralize Umar, Irish added silently.

"I'll stop by to see you after we're done here," Irish promised.

She gave him a tight smile. "I wouldn't dream of distracting you." Claire spun on her heels and left the room, closing the door behind her with a loud click.

"Sorry, Irish." Gator said. "You know as well as I do she would be in the way."

He sighed. "I know." Irish clapped his hands together. "Let's bring down Umar."

Claire really did understand why she'd been excluded from the operation planning. She didn't have the training and would be more of a liability than an asset.

Still, she wanted to be there for Dr. Jamo. But not at the expense of SEAL lives.

She sighed and walked back toward the clinic, curious about the courier and the role he played in the murder of the remote villagers.

The white truck stood where she'd originally found it, parked beside the clinic. At first, she didn't see the driver until he straightened at the tailgate.

Claire swung wide, noting that he'd shoved a box beneath a tarp in the bed of the truck.

The courier had his back to her, a cell phone sandwiched between his shoulder and ear. As he turned, he caught sight of her, his dark eyes narrowing, his gaze following her as she angled toward the clinic's front door.

A trickle of alarm dribbled down her spine. Claire hurried into the clinic and stood beside a window, staring out at the driver.

"May I help you?" asked the cheerful army female behind the counter.

"No, thank you." Claire shot a quick smile her way. "I'm waiting for someone."

"I don't blame you. The AC is nice in here."

Claire didn't respond, her gaze on the man standing outside the window in the alley between buildings.

He finished his conversation and walked away, leaving his truck unattended.

Her heart leaping into her throat, Claire opened the door to the clinic and peered out. She didn't see the courier anywhere. If she wanted to find out more about the box in the back of the truck, now was her chance.

"Have a nice day," the female soldier called out behind her.

Glancing right and left, she exited the building and hurried to the back of the vehicle and lifted the tarp. The box was made of hard plastic and had latches on the front. She flipped them loose and opened the box. Inside were vials of blood, packed in foam. The case was insulated from the heat. Nothing about the samples raised any alarm bells. As she closed the case and secured the latches, she wondered what she'd hoped to find.

The rattle of gravel warned her she wasn't alone. But before she could turn to face the man behind her, she felt a hand slam into her back, and she was thrown forward, banging her head against the hard plastic box. Stars swam before her eyes. When she tried to straighten, she felt a sharp prick of pain in her shoulder. Arms came around her body, clamping hers to her sides. She fought but she was no match for the superior strength of her opponent, and her muscles weren't cooperating.

Claire opened her mouth to scream. No sound passed her lips. The bright Djibouti sun snuffed out.

An hour later, Irish excused himself from the planning, his mind on Claire instead of the dangerous insurgency they planned. She'd left the room appearing to be angry at the way Tuck brushed her off. He couldn't blame her. At the same time, he hoped she'd get over it quickly, and they could pick up where they'd left off early that morning. The night ahead promised to be difficult and extremely dangerous. If they slipped up even a little, their weaknesses would be used by Umar to his advantage. The same way they felt about Umar, he'd feel about them. No prisoners would be taken. Umar would kill every last one of the SEALs if he had his way.

Their team's job was to see that didn't happen.

Irish headed for Claire's quarters, jogging in the heat to get there. She had to be champing at the bit to find out how things went in the briefing session. Not that he could give her specifics about the operation. Secrecy was vital to surprising the enemy.

One knock on her door resulted in no response. After the third knock, he grabbed the handle and twisted.

The door opened and a quick peek inside proved she wasn't there.

His stomach roiled, but Irish told himself not to worry. She was probably in the mess hall, getting lunch or a drink. With the desert sun beating down on him, he ran to the mess hall and burst through the door.

At a little past noon, the dining hall was teeming with soldiers, marines, sailors and air force personnel in PT gear or every pattern of desert camouflage. Irish searched for a blond-haired civilian among the military personnel.

"Looking for the pretty doctor?" Tuck stepped up behind him with the rest of the crew.

"Yeah. She wasn't in her quarters."

The group spent a couple minutes searching the sea of faces.

"I don't see her," Big Bird said.

"Neither do I," Tuck added.

The longer Irish looked, the worse he felt about the situation.

"You think she might have gone to the Post Exchange for clothes and toothpaste?"

"Maybe." Irish prayed that was where she'd gone. This post was bigger than some. Nevertheless, it shouldn't take long to find her.

"I hope I didn't piss her off too much by asking her to leave." Tuck clapped a hand on Irish's back. "Surely, she'll get over it."

"She's an adult, I doubt she'd take offense to being excluded from an operational planning session." At least Irish hoped she hadn't taken offense. He knew how much she cared about Dr. Jamo. She only wanted to see him rescued and freed from the clutches of a ruthless terrorist.

"I'll go check the Exchange," Tuck offered.

"I'll run by the shower facility," Dustman offered.

"Yeah, right." Swede laughed.

"I won't go in. I'll just stand outside and ask if anyone inside saw her." Dustman winked.

"I'm running back by the clinic," Irish said. "Being a doctor, she might have gone to check on the samples the courier had tested."

Tuck glanced at the watch on his wrist. "Meet back at my quarters in five minutes."

Every man looked at his watch, nodded and took off.

Irish arrived at the clinic a minute

later, having run the entire way. The white pickup was gone, and no one hung around outside in the heat. He opened the door and went inside.

"May I help you?" a female army private first class asked from behind the counter.

"Did a blonde come in here about an hour ago? She would have been wearing a dark T-shirt and blue scrubs."

The female tipped her head, touching her finger to her chin. "An hour ago, you say?"

Irish nodded.

The woman smiled. "Yes. She said she was waiting on someone."

"Did you see where she went when she left?"

"Not really. Maybe to the right, around the side of the building. I thought I saw someone out there through the window." The young woman gave him an apologetic smile. "Sorry."

Irish stepped outside and shaded his eyes to the sun. The right would have taken her to the pharmaceutical truck, if it had still been there. Holy hell, surely she didn't try to accost the courier? He hurried back to Tuck's quarters. All his worry would be for naught. One of the guys had to have located her at the Exchange.

Irish made it back to Tuck's place first. Even Tuck hadn't returned so he waited outside his quarters, pacing.

"Not at the Exchange," Tuck said behind Irish.

Dustman jogged up. "Dr. Boyette wasn't at the shower facility. I had a really hot lieutenant check to make sure."

Shoving a hand through his hair, Irish walked to the end of the row of housing containers and back. "Where would she be? Camp Lemonnier isn't that big."

"Do you think she left to find Dr. Jamo on her own?"

"How? She didn't have transportation to get there?"

"Could she have hitched a ride?" Tuck asked, his voice low, intense.

A lead weight settled in Irish's belly. "You mean with the courier?"

"We wouldn't let her go with us," Tuck said, shaking his head. "What would stop her from finding her own way out to where they could potentially have taken the Somali doctor?"

"Guys, we have to prepare for the mission tonight," Nacho said. "We'll keep our eyes open for her return."

"I'll show up in time to pack my gear. Until then, I'll be turning over every damned rock in this camp to find Claire."

Everyone took off to gather his gear,

except Swede. "Sorry about the doc. I hope you find her before we shove off." Then he gave Irish a hand-held electronic device. "In case she hitched a ride with the courier, you might want to keep this on you. Maybe he's headed to the same place we are." The big blond man pointed at a blinking dot on the screen. "He's already about sixty clicks from here and moving fast."

"Too fast to catch him?" Irish asked, his grip tightening on the device.

"Probably. Unless you could commandeer a helicopter to intercept."

The thought had crossed his mind, but the plan was to commandeer military aircraft for the unsanctioned mission that night. They could be in a whole lot of trouble for that if things didn't go well.

Irish drew in a deep breath and tamped down the urge to grab a vehicle and race after the courier. "I'll keep looking for her here."

"She'll turn up," Swede reassured him.

Irish sure as hell hoped she did. The alternative could get ugly.

Chapter Nine

CLAIRE DIDN'T AWAKEN until whatever it was she was bouncing on came to a stop, putting an end to the breeze keeping her relatively cool under the heavy blanket draped over her body.

Forcing open her eyes, she blinked several times. She couldn't remember going to sleep, and she didn't recognize where she was. Her head hurt and the heat was becoming unbearable beneath the blanket.

She tried to raise her hand, but her muscles felt heavy, listless and difficult to control. Persevering, she managed to capture the edge of the blanket only to realize it was a canvas tarp. Turning her head, she recognized a hard plastic case she'd seen before. Then the events came back to her. She'd been sneaking a peek into the back of the pharmaceutical courier's truck when something stuck her in the arm. The bastard had drugged her and shoved her into the truck bed. Hell, Irish would be beside himself.

Claire willed her muscles to work and tried to push to a sitting position. Footsteps in gravel sounded and the tailgate of the truck dropped with a metal clank.

Heart pounding, Claire rolled over, aiming to fall out of the back of the truck and run. Where? She had no idea. But sticking around wasn't an option. Anyone who would drug another person was bad. If he was connected in any way to Umar, her life expectancy would be short.

Concentrating all of her efforts, she rolled toward freedom.

Hands caught her before she hit the ground.

Facing the dirt, all she could see were a dozen dark feet in sandals and dark shoes, green, dusty trousers and more legs.

She was set on her feet, facing the courier. Then she turned, and her heart fell to the bottom of her stomach.

Umar stood among the dark-skinned men, glaring. "Woman, you have caused much trouble. I should have killed you long ago."

Though Claire shook inside at the sheer anger in his face, she responded, "If you had, you would be dead yourself."

His eyes narrowed, and his hand rose to press against his belly. "I think you poisoned me."

With nothing but bravado to defend herself, she lifted her chin. "You poisoned

yourself with evil. You have a black heart.
One day it will kill you."

He laughed out loud. "Big words for
one who will soon die." He jerked his
head and spoke swiftly in Arabic to the
courier.

The man grabbed her arm and jerked
her toward a walled compound.

As she entered through a guarded
gate, she looked up at an opulent palace
with four cylindrical turrets, one on each
corner. At the center of the structure, a
huge domed roof rose three stories into
the desert air. This had to be the palace of
Prince Yohannis.

Her pulse raced and hope blossomed.
If it was the palace, Dr. Jamo could be
somewhere inside. And the SEALs would
be on their way to this location that night
to free the good doctor and maybe Claire,
if Umar didn't decide she wasn't worth
keeping around.

She was led around the side of the
palace past guards dressed in dark green
uniforms, their heads swathed in dark
green cloth, carrying wicked-looking guns.
Claire shivered, praying the SEALs didn't
incur any casualties in their night raid. She
just had to find Dr. Jamo and hold out
long enough for a rescue.

The courier led her through a door
into the back of the palace and down

stone stairs to another door. A guard with a rifle guarded it. The courier spoke to him and then reached for what looked like a round steering wheel like those used to secure doors on a submarine. He turned it and a sucking sound ensued. Then the heavy door opened to a long tunnel-like corridor leading in what Claire guessed was away from the palace itself to an underground complex. Once they passed through, the guard secured the door behind them.

The long corridor opened into a larger room lined with doors and some glass walls overlooking what appeared to be laboratories. As she passed the glass windows, she could see people dressed in full body suits and hoods worn when working with hazardous materials. Her heart fluttered, and a sense of dread washed over here. This had to be the place they were developing the biological weapons.

The courier was met by yet another guard. He passed Claire off to him. The guard gripped her arm and shoved her toward a door, opened it and pushed her inside a small room with two cots pushed up against the walls.

A dark-skinned man rose to his feet, his eyes sad. "Oh, dear God. Dr. Boyette."

Claire walked toward him, tears

spilling down her cheeks. "Dr. Jamo, I'm so glad I found you."

He held up his hands and backed away. "I wish I could say the same. Unfortunately, you are now just as much a prisoner as I am. And worse."

"We'll get out of here," Claire insisted.

The door closed behind her with an ominous click, belying her words.

"It won't matter to me." Dr. Jamo stared at Claire. "I am infected with the disease they have been using to kill entire villages."

*

Night hadn't come soon enough. Irish spent the day combing the entire length of Camp Lemonnier. Each passing minute drove home the fact Claire was nowhere within the boundaries of the installation. The only hope he held onto was that the blip on the tracking device led to the very location they would hit on their mission to put an end to Umar and his reign of death.

Tuck leaned close in the back of the Black Hawk helicopter as they hovered over their landing position a mile away from their target, tucked in the rolling wasteland of the Ethiopian desert. "We'll get her out," he promised.

Irish nodded without speaking, his

entire focus on the mission ahead. He went over everything they'd learned about the palace, the lay of the land and the armed men they would encounter. Langley had come through with vivid satellite photos of the palace and what appeared to be air vents from an underground structure located to the east of the palace.

They'd deduced that if an underground laboratory existed, the entrance was either camouflaged or only accessible through the palace. Rather than hunt over the land for a hidden entrance, they'd chosen to slip into the palace and enter from there.

Intel also indicated the Ethiopian Prince Yohannis was not in residence at the time, lessening of a possibility of the raid creating an international incident.

Irish didn't give a rat's ass about the Ethiopian prince. If anything, he'd rather the prince was there so he could blow him up in the palace with his murderous comrade, Umar. Anyone in bed with Umar was equally evil and deserved to die. Experimenting with biological warfare on innocent villagers was beyond contemptible.

The helicopters hovered thirty feet above the ground, and the SEALs fast-roped to the ground and headed for the palace on the other side of the hill.

Irish had chosen to take point, anxious to get there, find Claire, kill Umar and blow up the entire operation. Between him and the others, they carried enough C-4 to take out an entire city block in downtown Manhattan.

Less than an hour was needed to climb the hill and slip up on the palace walls, surrounding it on all sides. Dustman, Nacho and two others had chosen positions farther out and set up as snipers while the rest of the sixteen-man team moved inside.

"There's a guard on each corner and one on the gate." Tuck's voice came through Irish's headset.

"Southeast target in my crosshairs," Dustman said.

"I've got the man on the gate," Nacho confirmed.

The other snipers reported in, targets acquired, awaiting orders to pull the trigger.

"You can bet security cameras will be in place. Once we move in range, we have to make it quick. Let's do this. Ready. Fire."

The soft crack of rifles going off at the same time could only be heard by someone listening really hard for the noise. The distance helped muffle the sound.

Irish watched through his night vision goggles as the guard nearest him slumped to the ground. The team moved in, breaching the gate, setting off a small explosion to trigger the automatic opener.

The SEALs hugged the inside of the outer wall and surrounded the palace.

Irish, Tuck, Big Bird, Fish and Swede approached the rear entrance. The rest of the team hung back to provide cover.

Tuck tried the door handle. Locked.

Prepared for this, Irish pressed a wad of C-4 near the locking mechanism and set a charge. The men took several steps away and covered their ears. A small explosion ripped through the lock, and the door swung open.

The SEALs waiting near the walls of the compound moved in.

With their MP5SD sound-suppressed submachine guns leading the way, the SEALs entered the building.

A guard came running around a corner, alerted by the sound of the blast.

Irish aimed for his knee. The bullet hit, sending the guard down, his rifle hitting the floor first, and then bouncing out of his grip.

Tuck rushed forward, kicked the rifle out of his reach and yanked him up by the back of his collar. In Arabic, Tuck demanded, "Where is Umar?"

The man shook his head, crying out in pain.

Tuck pulled his knife from the scabbard at his waist and pressed it to the man's throat, repeating his question.

Irish aimed his gun at the man's face as added incentive.

The al-Shabaab guard spoke haltingly.

Irish knew a little Arabic and gleaned the gist of the man's words. Umar was in a room upstairs.

"What about the doctors?" Irish urged.

Tuck translated.

Before answering, the guard wailed in pain.

The doctors were down the stairs in the laboratory.

Tuck nodded to Irish. "Take Big Bird and Swede. The rest will come with me to round up Umar and his thugs."

Without waiting for the others, Irish hurried along the hallway in the direction from which the guard had come. He came upon a stone staircase leading to a lower level.

"Go," Big Bird's voice said into his headset. "We've got your six."

Irish was already halfway down, moving silently. The staircase curved to the right. His training kicking in, Irish slowed, peered around the corner and noted a guard at the bottom of the stairs, standing beside a large door that reminded him of the ones on ships that could be shut airtight.

The guard spotted him about the same time. Before the man could raise his weapon, Irish fired and the guard dropped.

Grabbing the large round handle, Irish pulled it around, breaking the seal. The door swung open and the men raced down a long corridor. As they neared the end, an alarm sounded, and red lights blinked high on the walls.

Irish prayed Tuck and the others weren't running into trouble in the palace. Then he focused on the guard running toward him, eyes wide.

Irish dropped to his belly and fired a burst from his MP5SD, taking out the guard with the first bullet. The beauty of the sound-suppressed weapons was that they could fire in one room and not be heard in the next.

Unfortunately, the alarm system had every guard on alert.

Irish leaped to his feet and ran to the end of the hallway with Big Bird and Swede on his heels. More guards appeared, racing toward them. When they saw the SEALs, they raised their weapons.

Rolling to the side, Irish let loose another burst.

Big Bird and Swede joined in the fight.

The guards were no match for the Navy SEALs and hit the floor, blood pooling around their bodies.

Irish remained on his belly for a moment. When nothing moved, he rose, weapon at the ready. The room he'd entered was lined with doors on one side and glass walls on the other, overlooking a bay filled with tables, microscopes and people dressed in white hazmat suits. One look at the Navy SEALS and they dropped to the floor, covering their heads. Not one of them had weapons, but all of them were working on the most powerful weapons of all. The kind of weapon people couldn't see with the naked eye.

Pounding on a door near the end of the room caught Irish's attention. He hurried to the end and pressed his ear to the door. "Claire?"

"Irish!" Her muffled voice came through the thick door. "We're in here."

Relief flooded him as he twisted the handle. The door was locked. Rather than waste time searching through the dead guards for the key, he yelled, "Stand clear of the door and hold your ears." With a small clump of C4 and a detonator, he blasted through the lock, and the door swung open.

He would have rushed in, but Claire and Dr. Jamo both stood back, hands held up. "Don't come near us."

"Why?"

Dr. Jamo stood against the opposite wall from Claire. "I've been purposely infected with the virus they used in their bio warfare."

"I don't know if I'm infected. But it's best you stay at least three feet away."

"We have to get out of here," Irish said.

"It might be too late." Dr. Jamo coughed into his sleeve, his eyes glassy, his nose running. "The siren alerts everyone outside of the lab when the protocol has been breeched and the virus containment has been compromised. The laboratory is wired to self-destruct if the alarms are not reset within ten minutes. Everyone who is not in the lab is instructed to get out until the cause for the alert is contained."

"How did you find out about all this?" Irish asked.

"Umar is very proud of what he and Prince Yohannis have accomplished with this facility." Dr. Jamo snorted. "He liked bragging."

"We have to get out of here." Irish reached for Claire's hand. "Come on."

She avoided touching him and moved past him without breathing in his face.

Dr. Jamo nodded. "You must go first. If I do not make it out, it will not matter. I am a dead man."

Claire stopped and faced her friend, tears welling in her eyes. "Dr. Jamo, you have to come with us. We'll find a cure."

"Not in time to save me." He stood outside the door to his prison. "You must go. But be careful. If you have the virus, you could be spreading it to others."

Holding a hand to her chest, Claire nodded. "You're a good man and will be missed by your people."

"Go. I will ensure others do not leave and spread the disease."

"But the building will be destroyed."

He nodded. "And the plague of death will be destroyed with it."

"I can't go." Claire declared, walking toward Dr. Jamo. "I'm as contaminated as you are."

"No. It's spread by bodily fluids. You have not come in that close of contact." Dr. Jamo waved toward Irish. "Take her away, quickly."

Irish shouted to Swede and Big Bird who guarded the corridor into the laboratory. "Get out, now. This building is set to explode in less than ten minutes." Then he advanced on Claire. "You heard the doctor. You might not even be infected."

"We can't risk it," she said.

He didn't give her the choice. Bending low, he plowed his shoulder into her waist, tossing her over his shoulder in a fireman's carry. Then he raced after Big Bird and Swede to the end of the corridor.

The two SEALs waited at the airlock door.

"Keep going," Irish said. "Make sure the others extract. I'll get Dr. Boyette out."

"You might need help."

"We'll take our chances," Irish said.

"Irish," Tuck's voice came through his headset. "Our target has been secured. What's this about the building exploding?"

"If the alarms aren't shut down in ten minutes, the entire complex is rigged to detonate."

"Gotcha," Tuck said. "Bugging out."

"Irish, you're insane. Put me down." She squirmed within his hold.

"Not until we're out of the building." Irish climbed the stairs and headed for the rear exit.

"I can move on my own. You're putting everyone else at risk."

"I'm not leaving you inside," he said, his hold tightening on her legs. Those beautiful sexy legs that had been wrapped around him a few short hours ago. He refused to let those legs, this woman, be buried in this hellhole.

"Put me down." She pounded gently on his back.

He swatted her bottom, struggling to hold her as he reached the top of the stairs. "Shut up, woman. You're not changing my mind."

"Fine. You win. But let me help by carrying myself."

Breathing hard, he set her on her feet, grabbed her hand and ran for the door. "We're guessing D-minus two," he heard in his headset. "Everyone better be on their way out now."

Swede and Big Bird burst through the door first, clearing the perimeter.

Irish, several yards behind, hit the door, dragging Claire through. "We're not safe until we're well beyond the outer walls. Keep running," he yelled.

Claire did her best to keep up.

Out of the corner of his eyes, he noticed other SEALs pouring out of the front of the palace, racing for the gate.

Swede and Big Bird turned and leveled their weapons to provide cover.

Irish ran past the two men with Claire, determined to get her as far from the blast zone as possible. The high stone and concrete walls surrounding the compound would provide a good barrier, if they made it outside in time.

Irish didn't feel they were safe until he passed through the gate and put as much distance between them and the palace. He dragged Claire another hundred yards farther before he slowed, his heart pounding, breathing hard.

A rumble started deep in the ground.

Tuck and the remaining members of the team streamed through the gate as the explosions breeched the thick walls of the underground laboratory. More explosions erupted from inside the palace. The walls shook and then burst outward. The heavy, domed roof at the center shuddered then collapsed inward.

Irish pushed Claire to the ground and covered her body with his as rubble spewed from the buildings. He lay for a long while on top of her as dust and debris showered down. When the ground stopped shaking and the world went quiet again, he heard voices in his headset.

One by one the members of his team sounded off. Every last one of them had made it out alive.

Irish rolled off Claire and lay on his back. "Are you okay?"

She rolled over, too, her hair covered in a layer of dust. "For now." Claire turned to face him and glared. "You should have left me inside."

He came up on his elbow and leaned over her. "Nope."

"You could be infected with the virus. It kills."

"Then we'll die together." He bent and claimed her lips in a long, soul-defining kiss he couldn't have resisted had he tried. If this was the beginning of his end, he'd die a happy man, kissing the woman he knew in his heart he could love forever.

When he raised his head, he stared down into her eyes, illuminated by the moon struggling to shine through the cloud of dust hanging over the destroyed compound.

Claire raised a hand to his cheek. "You are insane."

"I couldn't leave behind the girl I want to date."

"About that…" She trailed a finger along his dusty cheek.

"Don't tell me you wouldn't go out with me if I was the last man on earth." He pressed a hand to his chest and heaved a big sigh. "Hearing that would completely crush me."

She chuckled. "No, I was going to say…I'm thinking of contacting Fish's girlfriend who has the floating doctor boat."

Irish's heart swelled. "Yeah?"

Claire smiled. "Assuming we make it out of Africa alive."

"You know she docks near Virginia Beach when she's not out doing her doctorly thing."

"I know." She stared up into his eyes. "There's a certain SEAL I was hoping to see when I'm in port."

"That SEAL better be me," he said, making his voice into a low growl.

"Can't think of one I'd love more." She reached up, cupped the back of his head and pulled him down to kiss her.

In the desert of Africa, Irish had met the woman who completed him. A brave, intelligent, amazingly beautiful woman who wanted to be with him as much as he wanted to be with her.

"Uh…" Tuck's voice crackled in his ear. "If you two are through playing kissy face, let's get out of here."

"Sorry," Irish said. "You'll have to send out the HAZMAT team. The doctor and I will need to be quarantined for fourteen days until we're cleared. We could have been exposed to the virus."

"Goddamn it, Irish. I give you one simple task and you fuck it up," Tuck teased.

"Not from where I'm standing, or sitting, or lying down." He bent and

captured Claire's lips again, kissing her,
loving every dirty, sexy inch of her, virus
and all.

Epilogue

"DINNER'S READY!" Claire called out from the kitchen. "Ummm." She turned and accepted a spoonful of seafood chowder from the chef. The explosion of flavors filled her mouth and made her want more.

Irish followed the delicious chowder with an equally delicious kiss.

"Where did you learn how to cook?" There were so many things Claire didn't know about this man she'd been with for the past month. Every time she thought she knew all his abilities, he surprised her with something new. Especially in the bedroom.

"I learned from me darlin' mum. The woman had a way with potatoes that could make a French chef cry."

"Remind me to thank her."

"You can thank her yourself. She's coming to visit next week."

"Next week?" Claire squeaked and stiffened. "I haven't found an apartment yet. You can't spring something like that on me."

"Why do you need to find another apartment? Aren't you comfortable here?"

Wide-eyed, she could only stare. "What will your mother think about you shacking up with a woman?"

"She'll be glad I've settled down." He handed her a set of oven mitts. "Some hungry men are waiting in there. If you'll carry the bread, I'll bring in the chowder."

"But what about your mother?"

"She's going to love you." He kissed the tip of her nose and handed her the basket of bread. "Just like I love you." Cupping the back of her head, he kissed her lips, his tongue sliding past her teeth to claim hers.

"Mmmm. Why did we invite your friends over when we could be enjoying this chowder all by ourselves?"

"Hey, I thought you two were feeding us." Fish appeared in the doorway with Natalie pulled against his side. He stopped and snorted. "Sheesh. Leave a man and a woman together in quarantine for a couple of weeks and this is what you get. Mush, mush and more mush."

Natalie laughed and took the breadbasket from Claire. "Where do we sign up for quarantine?"

Fish slid around Claire and Irish to collect the soup tureen. "Don't mind us. We'll just eat dinner while you two do your thing."

Her hands free, Claire locked them

behind Irish's neck and returned his kiss, her leg sliding up the back of his, desire spiking in the tiny kitchen of the apartment they'd shared since they returned Stateside after they'd been cleared of any viral infection.

Although Africa had been her home all her life, she'd discovered home was where the heart was and her heart had been captured by a strong, sexy, incredibly handsome Navy SEAL. And she wouldn't have it any other way.

The End

About the Author

Elle James *also writing as Myla Jackson* spent twenty years livin' and lovin' in South Texas, ranching horses, cattle, goats, ostriches and emus. A former IT professional, Elle is proud to be writing full-time, penning intrigues and paranormal adventures that keep her readers on the edge of their seats. Now living in northwest Arkansas, she isn't wrangling cattle, she's wrangling her muses, a malti-poo and yorkie. When she's not at her computer, she's traveling, out snow-skiing, boating, or riding her ATV, dreaming up new stories.

To learn more about Elle James and her stories visit her website at www.ellejames.com.

To learn more about Myla Jackson visit her websites at www.mylajackson.com

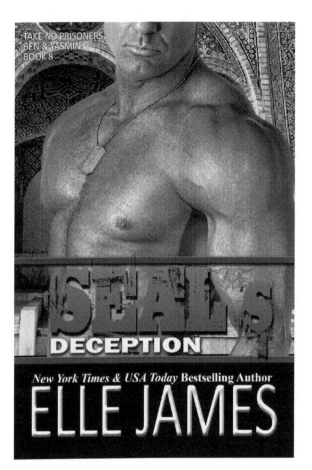

SEALS
DECEPTION

New York Times & USA Today Bestselling Author

ELLE JAMES

SEAL'S DECEPTION

TAKE NO PRISONERS

BOOK #8

ELLE JAMES

New York Times & USA Today
Bestselling Author

Chapter One

NAVY SEAL BEN "Big Bird" Sjodin had to duck his six-feet-six-inch frame to get through the door at Night Moves, the exclusive underground London nightclub. His contact with the CIA had some pretty impressive connections to get him cleared to enter. The poor son of a drunk from North Dakota had no business being in such a high-class establishment. Night Moves was the only place in the UK where the richest of the rich and the most popular celebrities gathered to drink, dance and partake of more exotic substances without the constant barrage of media and exuberant fans. Security was tight, and bodyguards swarmed the interior and exterior of the club to ensure the safety of the clientele.

Located in the heart of London, the building dated back to the seventeenth century and had sunk deeper into the ground over the years. Ben was used to ducking through doors. Having reached his full height at the age of fifteen, he'd had to be aware, or he'd end up with a constant lump on his forehead. Because of his height, he'd been called a lot of

1

things: String Bean, Jolly Green Giant, and Stretch. Names never bother him, not even the nickname with which his buddies on SEAL Team 10 had tagged him. What he didn't understand was why three members of his team had been deployed to conduct a covert operation in the exclusive underground nightclub. Stingray and Irish waited at a nearby pub, topside. Once Ben made contact with his CIA counterpart, he'd be led to a safe location to be briefed on the mission and what it entailed.

More familiar with combat missions in the deserts of Iraq and Afghanistan, he was left confused by the London nightlife, nearly blinded by the reflections off the sparkling diamonds gracing the necks of the ladies in the room. Fortunately, he'd been fitted for a tailored black suit, courtesy of the CIA, although the patent leather shoes weren't nearly as comfortable as his combat boots.

None of this operation made much sense. Since when did SEALs team up with the CIA for covert ops? And, without a gun, he felt damned near naked. At least he had his knife strapped to his calf beneath his trouser leg. Not that he expected a celebrity to start shooting. Hell, he doubted the rich and famous knew how to handle guns. However, several stern-faced bodyguards stood on the perimeter who looked like they ate nails for lunch.

They didn't bother Ben. He could take out any one of them with his hand-to-hand combat skills. When bullies targeted him in high school for being different, he'd fought back by bulking up and learning self-defense. His size helped establish him as the guy no one wanted to mess with, even keeping his father from slugging him whenever he was shit-faced drunk and ornery.

Ben found his way to the bar and waited for a seat to open. In the meantime, he ordered a glass of water. Had he been out with friends, he'd have gone for a beer, but tonight, he was working. Until he knew what the CIA had planned for him and his contact, he didn't dare imbibe. With an alcoholic father, Ben never drank more than he could handle. He had a terrifying fear of turning out just like his old man.

Leaning his back against the bar, he sipped the water and nearly spewed when bubbles tickled his nose. *Damn Europeans!* In what universe did a man order water and get some carbonated bullshit?

He set the glass on the counter with a thump and glared at the room full of beautiful people dressed to the nines, laughing, talking and dancing as if they hadn't a care in the world.

Ben tugged at the knot of his tie, wishing he was back in his T-shirt and blue jeans. If wearing a confining suit and shoes without traction was any indication of what the operation might be like, he had half a mind to call his commander back in Little Creek, Virginia, and tell him to find someone else.

A blonde, wearing a short red dress that fit so perfectly it could only have been painted on, stepped up to the bar and nodded to the bartender. "Water, please."

"Watch it. They don't serve water here," Ben muttered.

"What do you mean?" The woman turned his way.

At first, her accent sounded American, with a touch of English and a flair of something Ben couldn't quite put his finger on—Turkish, or maybe Middle Eastern.

"It has bubbles," he warned. "If you don't like bubbles in your water, order something else."

She smiled. "It's sparkling, and that's the only way I drink virgin water." While she waited for the bartender to fill her glass, she turned to Ben. "You're an American, aren't you?"

He nodded, not really interested in continuing the conversation.

"Where in the U.S.?" she persisted.

Her voice was warm, like syrup pouring over his skin, melting into his pores. Ben tugged at his tie again, inclined to move away, afraid if he got started talking to the gorgeous woman, he wouldn't want to stop. He wasn't there to chat with a beautiful socialite; he was there to connect with an operative. "From all over," he said noncommittally, searching the crowd for anyone who might look like a CIA spy. Shit, what did a CIA spy look like? All this covert bull was well out of his league.

The bartender set a glass of sparkling water on the counter top.

The woman lifted it and touched her full, lush lips to the rim.

Ben's gaze followed, his groin tightening. Though she had blond hair, her brows were dark and her skin tones were more exotic. Blond or brunette, it didn't matter. She was striking and knew how to use her body to illicit a response. Yeah, and his body was responding. Damn!

He didn't need this distraction. If he was there to drink, maybe, but he wasn't. He was working. Ben straightened and took a step away.

Her hand shot out to clutch his arm. "Oh, don't go. Things were just starting to get... stimulating."

"Pardon me, ma'am. But I'm not interested." Ben peeled her hand off his arm and, again, started to walk away.

The woman's lips pressed together. She planted herself in front of him and walked her fingers up his chest. "Oh, come on, darling. Don't be such a spoilsport." She traced a line down his chest and snagged his hand. "Dance with me."

Once she had his hand in hers, she didn't let go. And her grip was surprisingly strong, for a woman. Instead of prying her fingers loose and raising a ruckus, Ben allowed himself to be dragged toward the dance floor and into the woman's arms. His gaze slipped around the room, still unable to detect which man might be his contact. Rather than fight off the woman, he figured he'd blend in with the crowd and have a better chance of spotting someone from his position in the middle of the room. He relaxed against her, moving to the music but ready to react at any given second.

Although tall and gangly as a teen, he'd always had a natural rhythm and moved well on the dance floor. He never lacked for a partner and often had his pick of the ladies for mattress dancing later. But Ben never stayed the night, always preferring to go back to his own place, rather than pretend a night in the sack meant anything by the next morning.

Long-term relationships weren't for him. And, God forbid, he should ever spawn children. With a drunk for a father, and a mother who hadn't loved him enough to take him with her when she ran out, Ben would bet his genes were hardwired to be a lousy parent. Why inflict bad genes on a kid?

The woman in his arms rubbed every part of the front of her body against his, straddling his thigh several times in what Ben could only assume was an attempt to have sex on the dance floor. When he glanced around at the other dancers, he noted they were all pretty much doing the same.

"Sweetheart, loosen up." She wrapped her arms around his neck and mashed her breasts to his chest. "You're so stiff." Her calf slid up the back of his leg and her sex pressed against the top of his thigh. "Mmm...hard in all the right places." She leaned up on her toes, stretching to plant a kiss on his lips. "And so tall." Her fingers threaded through his hair, and she dragged down his head, making it easier for her to nibble his earlobe. "I've been waiting for a guy like you." She leaned back in his arms and glanced around the room. "Ever been to Africa, big boy? Wanna go to my place and get wild?"

Ben stopped in the middle of the floor. The code word for his contact was Africa. Body tensed, he frowned at his dance partner. "Been there. Done that. Got the scars to prove it," he replied with the required response he hadn't had to rehearse. Ben *had* been to Africa, and had scars from gunshot wounds to prove it.

He'd been to Somalia not long ago with his SEAL team. They'd gone in to decapitate the head of a Somali rebel group. When the operation went south, he and his team had been lucky to get out alive.

"Mmm. You can show me your scars, and I'll show you mine." She took his hand and led him across the floor, heading for the exit. Halfway there, she came to an abrupt halt.

Ben bumped into her.

"On second thought, I think another drink is in order." The woman changed directions and tugged him toward the bar. "Things just might get interesting around here."

As she reached the counter, she nodded to the bartender. "I'll have the

Saturday Night Special."

The bartender glanced across the room, reached beneath the counter, pulled out a bottle of Jack Daniels whiskey, poured two shots and pushed them across the counter toward them. He wiped the bar behind the shot glasses and left the towel.

The blonde handed a shot to Ben, took the other and nodded. "Here's to getting to know you." She tossed back the whiskey in one swallow, grabbed the towel on the counter and spun toward the door.

A man entered, wearing a long black trench coat, his arm plastered to his side.

From the bar, Ben had a clear view of the doorway and the man coming through. He acted as if he had something beneath his coat, either strapped to his leg or resting against it. Alarm bells rang out in Ben's head.

"I'll take the trench coat, if you'll get the guy by the stage," the woman said.

"What guy?" Ben snapped his gaze to the stage where another man in a similar trench coat stood, his eyes narrowed, his arm against his side.

Fuck.

They carried rifles.

Ben nodded. "Deal. If you'll excuse me, I have some business to take care of." He clapped a hand around the woman's

9

neck, dragged her in for a quick, hard kiss and released her. "Let's get wild later."

"You got it. In the meantime, knock yourself out." She moved toward the exit.

About the time the two men nodded toward each other and parted the lapels of their trench coats, Ben and the woman were on them.

"Got a light, mate?" Ben stepped directly in front of his guy, so close the man couldn't bring up the rifle beneath his coat.

"Bug off," the man said, attempting to step around him.

Again, Ben planted himself in front of the man. "Just asked a simple question. You don't have to get so…" He swung his elbow, catching the man's nose in a sharp upward thrust.

The guy grunted, and blood spurted from his nose.

"I'm sorry, did I hurt you?" Ben asked. "Here, let me help." He placed a hand on the man's shoulder and shoved him down hard while bringing his knee up at the same time. Again, he hit the man in the face.

Too stunned to do much more than stagger backward into the stage, the man fumbled with the rifle beneath his coat.

Ben yanked the trench coat over his shoulders, trapping the man's arms to his sides. The rifle fell to the ground, the clattering sound drowned by the loud music.

With a quick kick, Ben sent the rifle beneath the closest table before twisting the coat up behind the man's back and glancing toward the front entrance. He didn't see the other man in the matching trench coat, nor did he see the woman who'd downed whiskey like Kool-Aid.

The wealthy men and women in the room only gave him fleeting glances as they twisted and gyrated to the music or went back to sniffing the lines of white powder on the glass-topped tables.

A bulky bodyguard narrowed his eyes and moved toward Ben.

Before the bodyguard could reach him, a woman teetered forward, bumping into the man Ben held in a vice grip

"Pardon me." She did a double take at the guy Ben was pushing through the crowd. She poked a finger into the man's chest and slurred, "You should have that looked at. You're bleeeeding." With a giggle, she twirled around and ended up on the dance floor, joining the other patrons moving to a techno-beat.

As he neared the door with his captive, Ben stopped short.

A group of people backed into him, and a woman screamed.

Rather than let go of the man he had in tow, Ben slammed the guy's face into a table, effectively knocking him out. He planted a chair over him and shoved a young man into it. "Stay here until I come back to collect."

The young man's head lolled, and he grinned. "Right."

Shoving his way through the gawkers, Ben found the woman in the red dress lying on the floor with the other man in the trench coat, her thighs wrapped around his throat, squeezing hard.

The rifle he'd carried in lay nearby. Thankfully, no one had picked it up.

"Need a hand?" he asked the woman.

"No. I got this covered. You might secure his weapon."

As Ben reached for the rifle, a burly bodyguard grabbed it first.

"If you know what's good for you, you'll give me that weapon." Ben nodded to the woman on the ground. "Otherwise, I'll turn my girlfriend loose on you."

The lady in the red dress unwound her legs from the man's throat, stood and smoothed her dress over her hips. "I'll take that, Wendell." She held out her hands.

The bodyguard placed the rifle in them, giving Ben a fierce glare. "Yasmin, you know this fella?" The bodyguard handed over the rifle and jerked a thumb toward Ben.

She grinned. "You heard him, he's my boyfriend."

Ben didn't know what the operation was all about, but he did know that the men they'd subdued had come into the club with the intent to fire off enough rounds to decimate the clientele. Had Yasmin not noticed them when she had, potentially every man and woman cavorting on the dance floor would have left the building in body bags.

Wendell gave a single nod toward Yasmin. "Thanks, lady. Anytime you need anything, you just call."

Her grin faded into a serious look. "I'm counting on it."

A couple other bouncers converged on Ben, Yasmin and the two attackers.

"We'll clean up the mess," Wendell said. "You might want to get out of here before the Bobbies arrive."

Yasmin gave the bouncer one last glance, hooked Ben's arm, and led him out of the club onto the cool, damp street in London.

"Did you know those men would be there?" Ben asked.

"I had received reasonably reliable intel they might make their move tonight. My counterparts didn't believe me." She shrugged and turned right, stepping out with purpose. "Guess they were wrong."

Ben hurried to catch up, curious about this woman who could choke the life out of a man with her thighs, get up and walk away like it was part of her normal exercise routine. For all he knew, that move could be.

"Do you mind telling me who you are, and why the Navy SEALs have been tasked to work with a former INTERPOL, now CIA, agent on a covert operation?"

"When we get to a safe location, I'll tell you what I know. In the meantime, keep your eyes open. Those two gunmen probably weren't the only ones scheduled to attack."

An explosion rocked the streets several blocks from where they were.

Ben stopped and spun toward the sound.

Yasmin's hand on his arm halted him before he could run toward the noise. "It's already done. There's not much you can do to help those people. By the time you get there, the police and ambulances will have arrived. You'll only be in the way." She took his hand. "Come on. We have an operation to kick off and no time to waste."

As if to emphasize her prediction, the

wail of sirens sounded in the distance. People emerged from buildings, stared at the skyline and huddled in groups, whispering.

Ben tapped his ear bud communication device. "Connected with my contact. Moving to a safe location. Will report in when I know more."

"You weren't part of that explosion we heard, were you?" Irish asked.

"No," Ben said. "It wasn't anywhere close to us."

"Good to know," Irish responded. "So who's your contact?"

"I'll tell you when I know more," Ben said.

"Ha!" Stingray interjected. "He's a she. You dog. I'll bet she's gorgeous. Tell us where you are. I want to meet this sweet thing."

Ben tapped the ear bud several times. "You're breaking up. Contact you when I can."

"Breaking up my ass—" Stingray said as Ben turned off the earbud.

Yasmin glanced over her shoulder without slowing. "Your teammates?"

"Yup."

"I take it you're on a tracker, too." She ducked down an alley between buildings.

Ben hurried after her. "Yup."

15

"They'll follow."

Probably. As little as Ben had revealed, they'd be too curious to wait for him to give a location. Stingray and Irish would have the handheld tracker on by now. Ben's lips quirked upward. They'd be surprised by the beautiful woman they'd find him with. And, if they tried to sneak up on him, he might have the pleasure of watching her kick their asses.

Other Titles by Elle James

Demon Series
Hot Demon Nights (#1)
Demon's Embrace (#2)
Tempting the Demon (#3)

Protecting the Colton Bride
Heir to Murder
Secret Service Rescue
Tarzan & Janine
Haunted
Wild at Heart
Engaged with the Boss
Cowboy Brigade
Time Raiders: The Whisper
Bundle of Trouble
Killer Body
Operation XOXO
An Unexpected Clue
Baby Bling
Nick of Time
Under Suspicion, With Child
Texas-Sized Secrets
Alaskan Fantasy
Blown Away
Cowboy Sanctuary
Lakota Baby
Dakota Meltdown
Beneath the Texas Moon

71622187R00110

Made in the USA
Middletown, DE
26 April 2018